GOLD'S GYM GUIDE TO FITNESS

TRAIN FOR STRENGTH

THE EXPERTS AT GOLD'S GYM

Enslow Publishing
101 W. 23rd Street
Suite 240
New York, NY 10011
USA
enslow.com

This edition published in 2019 by Enslow Publishing, LLC.
101 W. 23rd Street, Suite 240, New York, NY 10011

Cataloging-in-Publication Data

Names: The Experts at Gold's Gym.
Title: Train for strength / The Experts at Gold's Gym.
Description: New York : Enslow Publishing, 2019.
| Series: Gold's Gym guide to fitness | Includes glossary and index.
Identifiers: ISBN 9781978506831 (pbk.) | ISBN 9781978506565 (library bound)
| ISBN 9781978506848 (6-pack)
Subjects: LCSH: Weight training—Juvenile literature. | Muscle strength—Juvenile literature.
| Weight lifting—Juvenile literature. | Physical fitness—Juvenile literature.
Classification: LCC GV546.2 O949 2019 | DDC 613.713—dc23

Printed in the United States of America

To Our Readers: We have done our best to make sure all website addresses in this book were active and appropriate when we went to press. However, the author and the publisher have no control over and assume no liability for the material available on those websites or on any websites they may link to. Any comments or suggestions can be sent by e-mail to customerservice@enslow.com.

Photo credits: All Gold's Glow Photography courtesy of Gold's Gym, with the following exceptions: ICON Health and Fitness (p. 28 bottom left, 30 left, 34); RFE International Ltd. (p. 14 bottom, 28 bottom right).

All other photos courtesy of Shutterstock.com: antoniodiaz (p. 12–13, 34); ARENA Creative (p. 11 bottom); ArtRoms (p. 23 top); Paul Biryukov (p. 16); didesign 021 (p. 30 bottom); GlebStock (p. 21); holbox (p. 23 bottom); Jasminko Ibarkovic (p. 39); Lucky Business (p. 10 top); Master1305 (p. 44 bottom); Sergey Nivens (p. 27 top); Skydive Erick (p. 26 bottom); Syda Productions (p. 7, 10 bottom, 20, 24–25, 38); David Tadevosian (p. 21); VGstockstudio (p. 34–35); wavebreakmedia (p. 42–43).

All exercise instructional illustrations by Remie Geoffroi.

All anatomical illustrations by design36/Shutterstock.com, except p. 8–9 by jovan vitanovski/Shutterstock.com.

All other illustrations courtesy of Shutterstock.com: pking4th icon in upper right corner headings.

CONTENTS

AMERICAN 100 BARBELL
GOLD'S GYM
TEAM

INTRODUCTION

Resistance training is a key part of any fitness regimen. It not only increases strength, power, and endurance, it also tones muscles and can make them larger. Making resistance training a part of your regimen has other benefits, too.

APPRECIATE THE BENEFITS

A resistance workout acts as a major metabolism booster because the body continues to burn far more calories after a strength session than after aerobic exercise. When training is done through a full range of motion, it will improve flexibility, renew fluidity, and reduce the risk of injuries, muscle pulls, and back pain. It also improves posture, aids balance and coordination, and can prevent loss of muscle mass. Its results also work wonders on your self-image and state of mind. There are indications resistance training can even enhance cognitive function. Healthwise, resistance training can reduce resting blood pressure, help control blood sugar, and improve cholesterol levels. Studies indicate that resistance training can positively affect insulin sensitivity, resting metabolic rate, body fat, glucose metabolism, blood pressure, and gastrointestinal transit time, and reduce risk factors for diabetes, heart disease, and cancer.

CHOOSE THE METHOD

At Gold's Gym, you'll find a wide range of strength-building tools—resistance-based machines such as the leg press or the pec deck, or hand-held free weights like barbells, dumbbells, and medicine balls. You can even exercise without implements or tools, using your own body weight to create resistance. Depending on whether your goal is to increase muscle size or build strength, your training volume—the number of reps per set—will differ. To gain size, you need to stress the muscle by upping the volume of reps per set, while maintaining an optimum amount of weight. If you want to focus on strength, your volume of reps per set will be less, but you will work with increased weight.

FOLLOW THE PROGRAM

When augmented by a healthy diet and a cardiovascular exercise program, resistance training can benefit your life every single day. Whether it's carrying grocery bags from the car, engaging in your favorite recreational sports, or simply fighting off the encroachments of aging, a regular strength regimen that burns fat, builds muscle, and stabilizes your skeletal system will leave you feeling fit, energized, and confident.

START RESISTANCE TRAINING

Many of us who are new to the gym experience, or who simply want to get fit, may ask a trainer, "Why get involved in weight training or bodybuilding?" A wise pro will be quick to point out the numerous benefits of resistance work, or "pumping iron," as enthusiasts call free-weight exercise. The advantages include increasing one's bone density, enhancing the shape of the body, and improving posture and functionality. Weights are also the key to giving yourself a customized workout by augmenting your own natural shape and musculature—resistance training allows you to pinpoint each muscle group with precise, controlled movements. This can result in better muscle definition and, with dedication and time, a truly sculpted physique. In fact, there is such an extensive list of positive attributes that not investigating resistance training in some capacity is like having a sporty car but no fuel.

COMPARE YOUR OPTIONS

The three main tools of resistance training are free weights, resistance machines, and your own body weight. Resistance machines are the weight machines, like the leg press or lat pull-down, that target specific areas of the body. Hand-held free weights, such as barbells, dumbbells, kettlebells, and medicine balls, allow for a wide range of motion. Exercises that use your own body weight for resistance, a practice sometimes referred to as calisthenics, are aid free. Each method has its advocates, but there are also certain drawbacks. This table explains some of the pros and cons.

MODALITY	PROS	CONS
RESISTANCE MACHINE	Ideal for beginners	Restricts range of motion
	Encourages proper form	Does not work ancillary muscles
	Follows predetermined resistance path	Popular machines may be in heavy rotation
FREE WEIGHT	Allows full range of motion	May require a spotter
	Develops ancillary muscles	Dismounts can be risky
	Easily utilized at home	Users need to work up to compound lifts
BODY WEIGHT	No equipment needed	No way to increase resistance
	Exercise anywhere, any time	Isolating certain muscles is tricky
	Builds strength, flexibility, and mobility	Less ability to build mass, especially in legs

CALCULATE THE NUMBERS

If you are a novice heading for the resistance machines or the weight room, the first thing you probably think is, "How much weight should I aim for?" and then, "How many reps and sets should I perform?" Although there is no one formula for determining the ideal weight or perfect number of reps and sets for a given machine or exercise, there are some useful guidelines. Getting close to the right numbers could be the difference between a successful session with great results and wasted time on the gym floor.

When you begin, choose weights that are light enough so that you can do 12 to 17 reps over two to three sets—but only do 10 to 12 reps initially. Those extra reps are "in the tank"—meaning you could do them, but don't want to push your muscles yet. You don't want to shock your brain or nervous system with a searing workout, not until they figure out how to properly coordinate the movements the exercise requires. In order to concentrate on your form, start with two sets of 12 reps or three sets of 10 reps. Your nervous system will soon learn which muscle fibers to contract and which to relax. Your muscles themselves will adapt to the workload. At about two weeks, speak to a trainer about increasing your weight load, performing fewer reps, but adding more sets.

LEARN THE WORKOUT BASICS

There are varying levels of definition—the visible development of muscles—that gym-goers hope to achieve, from simple toning to competitive bodybuilding. If you want to gain bulk along with body conditioning, consider a combination of speed lifting, interval training, and supersets. This is especially true if you want to achieve that "ripped" look of extreme muscle definition. If you seek to improve strength but not size, try short rep workouts using extra-heavy lifts. The logic behind this is that the less amount of time a muscle is stressed, the less likely it will be to expand in size.

To utilize resistance training properly, there are a number of factors you need to understand.

WARM-UP AND COOL-DOWN Whether you choose cardio or stretches before or after resistance training, leave time for properly warming up and cooling down.

TYPE OF LIFT Tailor your workouts to focus on specific body areas, especially the ones that might be problematic.

PROGRESSIVE OVERLOAD By gradually increasing your weights, your muscles will grow larger and stronger.

INTENSITY The weight as a percent of your one-rep max.

FREQUENCY The ideal frequency of workouts varies depending on each individual, but most people see the best results with three to four resistance-training sessions per week, never working the same muscle group two days in a row.

VOLUME This usually refers to the total number of sets and reps completed within a specified time period. Can be categorized by muscle groups or areas of the body.

VARIETY Switching the order of exercises (or the exercises themselves), rep schemes, or training volumes challenges your muscles, which will adapt by increasing their strength and size.

REST How long you rest between sets affects your results: 30- second to 60-second breaks increase muscle size and endurance; rests of two to four minutes result in strength alone.

RECOVERY Muscles need time to repair and grow after a workout. Try to allow 48 hours of recovery before re-working the same group.

WORKOUT APPS

Various fitness apps help you set and track your goals, join fitness groups, share ideas, and get advice. Others show exercises or guide you through various routines with step-by-step instructions, features to function as a personal trainer. Gold's Gym myPATH works with most fitness trackers, recording calories burned, workout duration, reps, and more, all in real time.

- *Gold's Gym myPATH*
- *CARROT Fit*
- *Daily Burn*
- *Fitocracy*
- *FitStar*
- *Jefit Workout*
- *The Johnson & Johnson Official 7 Minute Workout*
- *Pocket Yoga*
- *Progression*
- *Sworkit*
- *Touchfit: GSP*
- *Workout Trainer*

KNOW YOUR MUSCLES

Before you begin a resistance-training program, it's a good idea to familiarize yourself with the basics of your musculature. These illustrations provide a quick visual guide to the major muscle groups that you will be targeting during workouts. For more detailed information on their functions, see the individual tips indicated after the muscle names.

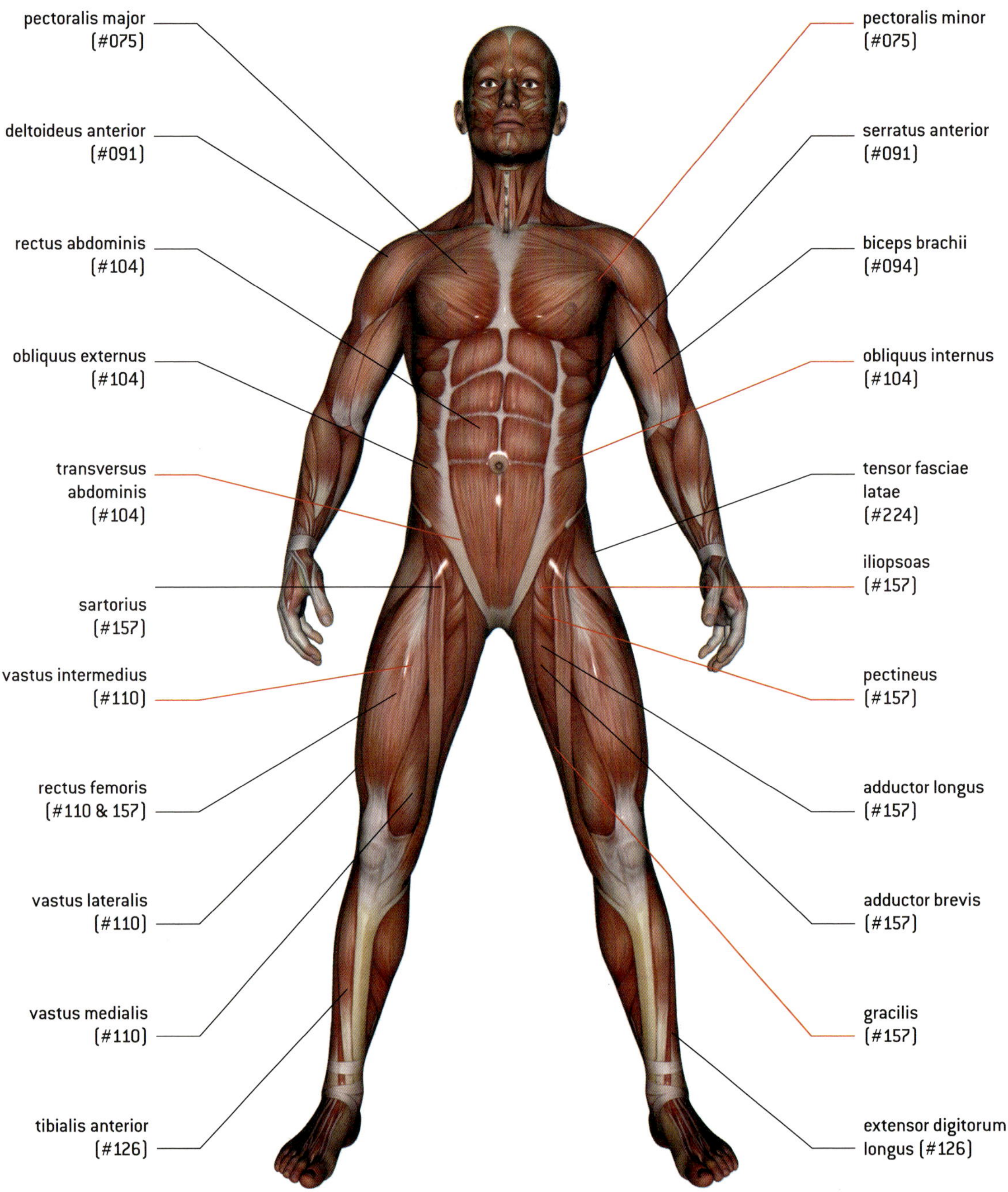

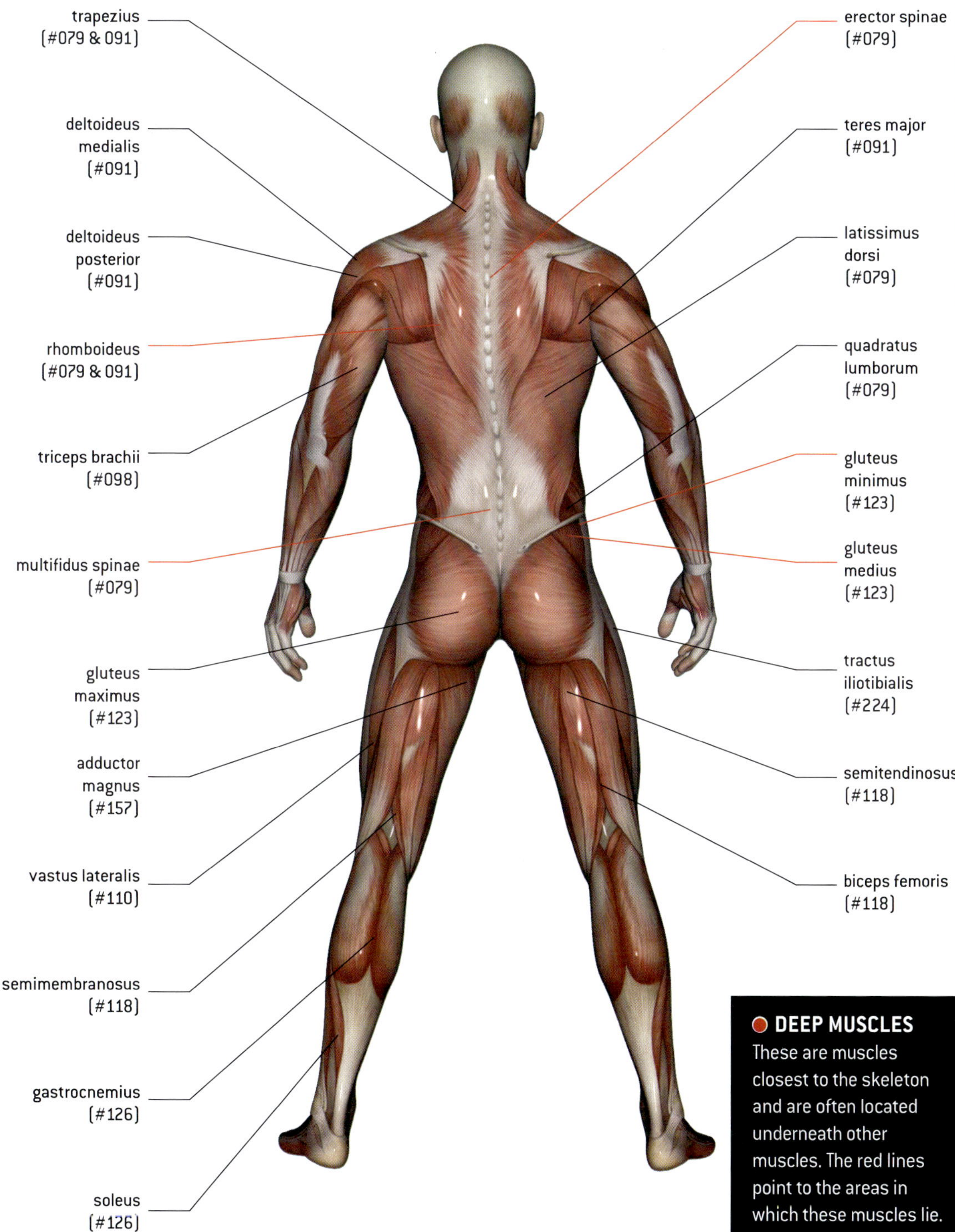

DEEP MUSCLES

These are muscles closest to the skeleton and are often located underneath other muscles. The red lines point to the areas in which these muscles lie.

Ask the EXPERT

HOW DO MUSCLES GROW?

Muscle hypertrophy, or increased size of skeletal muscle, is the body's adaptive stance when increased resistance or force is placed upon the body. The number of muscle cells does not increase, but rather their size does. Resistance training generally results in two types of growth: sarcoplasmic hypertrophy and myofibrillar hypertrophy. The former focuses more on increased muscle glycogen storage and is found in professional bodybuilders and endurance athletes. The latter, which focuses more on increased myofibril (the rodlike unit of a muscle cell) size, is seen in powerlifters, Olympic lifters, and strength athletes. These two factors do not occur in isolation, with the result that both bodybuilders and strength competitors differ little in strength and muscle size. For the average gym-goer, a consistent progressive overload, whereby you increase the resistance and/or repetitions, will aid in muscle hypertrophy.

MASTER MUSCLE CONTROL

When learning to perform an exercise, you'll often hear the instruction to engage a particular muscle or muscle group—a task that sounds easier than it is. This is muscle control, or the ability to voluntarily flex or relax specific muscles. This calls for a deep connection between your mind and body.

During an exercise, you contract certain muscles in groups or in isolation, which causes the weight to move. Learning to target the correct muscles takes practice, however. For example, when executing a biceps curl, a neophyte will pick up a dumbbell, curl upward, and feel some sensation in the biceps , but also in the forearms and even the anterior deltoids because these muscles are all programmed to get the weight up. To practice control, forget about the lift and instead focus your mind on the contraction and relaxation of particular muscles. Beginners will be sure to feel other muscles come into play. For example, try to isolate the contraction of your latissimus dorsi (the large muscle on either side of your back). You'll probably feel your chest and shoulders muscles also contract.

To learn true muscle control, you must master two important actions: relaxation and contraction.

FULL-BODY RELAXATION Learning to engage a muscle also means learning to relax it. To practice this skill, stand tall and consciously look for tension in any muscle, and then relax it. With time and practice, you'll eventually be able to consciously relax a muscle without contracting those nearby.

FULL-BODY CONTRACTION After practicing relaxation, try for full-body contraction. Again stand tall, but now try to contract all of your muscles simultaneously. Keep your breath shallow while contracting, and pay attention to your body. You may believe that every muscle is fully contracted, but you've likely missed some that are not under proper control. As with the relaxation exercise, scan your body from head to toe to note any muscles you have missed, and contract them. Make sure that no other muscles relax while doing this.

Working on mastering your muscles will allow you to focus less upon lifting heavy weights during resistance training and focus more on feeling the muscles that are doing the work.

GYM *etiquette*

ASK AN EXPERT

If you notice another gym-goer whose body condition inspires you, or if you have questions on how others reached their goals—goals that you would also like to achieve—simply ask them. Just be sure it's after their workout or while they are resting; it's bad gym etiquette to interrupt anyone during a workout. Most will be flattered that you noticed the result of their hard work and will be happy to offer you assistance and advice when approached in the proper way.

You can also ask for recommendations on specific personal trainers—who works well with those at your level of expertise, for instance, or their opinion of various classes. At the very least you will come away with some useful new knowledge, and (even better) you may have gained a new friend or workout buddy.

TOOLS of the TRADE

BRING ON THE BARBELLS

The standard barbell might just be the quintessential piece of resistance-training equipment, so it's smart to familiarize yourself with this tool. Length varies, but a typical bar is about 7 feet (2 m). Even before you add any weight plates, the bar comes in at about 45 pounds (20 kg). Quality varies, but a good steel bar should be able to hold a lot of poundage. Knurling—or grooving—on the bar allows for a better grip. Standard bars are best for squats, overhead presses, and bent-over rows.

Thickness and the amount of whip—the ability to bend a bit and rebound—are two ways to differentiate specialty bars. A thick squat bar has very little whip and also has knurling at its center to help grip the back of your shirt so that it doesn't slide. A narrow deadlift bar has a bit more whip, which gives it greater speed off the floor. Bars for bench presses are slightly thicker with almost no whip, allowing for a more stable exercise.

SPOT YOUR PARTNER

Spotting—staying close by someone who is working with weights and watching out for any potential danger or fumbles—is a key way to put safety first at the gym. Here are several things you should keep in mind when spotting your workout partner or a gym buddy.

DO Always prioritize the lifter's safety.

DON'T Do not grab the bar until necessary.

DO When spotting on the barbell bench press, place yourself high enough so that you can grab the bar in any position. And be sure to grab the bar with a double overhand grip. If you have to touch the bar, the lifter should end with that particular rep.

DON'T Do not spot a barbell squat by trying to grab the bar (unless there is a spotter at each end of the bar).

DO When spotting dumbbell movements, always spot from the wrist. Don't push on the elbows to help finish a chest lift. Spot a lunge or a squat from behind, with your arms under your partner's armpits; wrap your arms around your buddy's chest, and lift him or her into a stand. Once you are experienced, a trainer may move around to check your form from all angles, but for all weight moves, learn the best angle to stand at and how to correctly spot your partner.

DON'T Do not spot someone who is attempting a deadlift, clean, snatch, or overhead press. It is too dangerous for both individuals. The lifter should have learned the technique to safely execute—and disengage from—these advanced lifts before attempting them.

COMPLETE THE REP

There are a number of theories on repetition performance ... some experts recommend going slowly, others advocate speed. Perhaps it helps to understand how repetitions work.

THE NEGATIVE During each rep, there is a negative, which means the muscle lengthens (as the biceps brachii does when you lower your arm during the downward motion of a biceps curl, for example).

THE POSITIVE The negative portion of a rep is followed by a positive portion (the upward flexion, or shortening motion, of the biceps during the curl).

THE STATIC Once you have performed the positive portion of the rep, until you move back down into the negative portion, the muscle will then remain static in the contracted position.

Strength-building muscle breakdown happens mostly during the negative phase, so it is critical to complete the full range of motion in order to develop the muscle. You should perform the reps of most exercises with a controlled negative and a more explosive positive for maximum effect, and always work with weights you can handle.

BREATHE IN, BREATHE OUT

There are times when breathing becomes more complicated in the course of working out than it needs to be. Ideally, you want to breathe in on the negative movement—the lowering of the weight—and exhale on the positive—or working—portion of the repetition. Breathe in as you lower the barbell in a bench press, for instance, and exhale as you push it back up.

WORK TO FAILURE

The gym is perhaps one of the few places where failure is welcome. "Failure"—the inability to do even one more rep—means you've exhausted a muscle to the point where it can temporarily no longer move. Over time, muscle failure coupled with increased lifts and good nutrition will result in larger, firmer, and stronger muscles.

WATCH YOUR FORM

Any time you lift weights, you put stress on your back. Paying attention to your form can help you ensure that your workout remains safe and beneficial.

CONTROLLED WEIGHT Make sure to control the weight at all times. Don't swing free weights up and down or allow momentum to drive your movements.

CORRECT TECHNIQUE Ensure that you move the weight through your joint's full range of motion. This not only completely works the muscle, it also reduces the risk of joint injury. If you are unsure of what the proper technique is, consult a qualified trainer or physiotherapist. Incorrect technique can slow your progress or even cause injuries.

WEIGH IN ON WEIGHT BELTS

There are both proponents and detractors of weight-lifting belts. Pro lifters proudly wear specialized belts, yet many folks brag that they never do. The consensus seems to be on the positive side, but you must decide based on your own criteria. Naturally, if you have back or spinal issues, discuss the belt option with a trainer or physiotherapist.

PRO Belts stabilize and reduce stress on the spine. Research confirms that wearing a belt during lifting increases intra-abdominal pressure by as much as 40 percent. This can be compared to inflating a balloon inside your abdominal cavity—the pressure supports your spine from the inside, while the core muscles of the abdominal wall and lower back push on the spine from the outside. It is not so much about the belt providing spinal support, as that the body reacts to wearing the belt in a supportive manner.

PRO Belts aid body biomechanics. Studies also show that wearing a belt while lifting from the ground reduces spinal flexion, spinal extension, and lateral flexion. However, it also increases flexion at the hips and knees. In effect, a belt forces your lower body—legs and hips—to do the lifting, rather than your more vulnerable back. This biomechanic effect is especially important during deadlifts and squats with barbells.

PRO Belts improve performance. Many weight lifters say that wearing a weight belt improves power, strength, and muscle growth, most evidently in lower-body exercises.

CON Belts mean a loss of impact. There are those who believe that weight-lifting belts prevent strengthening of the lower back and possible inhibition of motor learning in the abdominals.

If you do decide to wear a weight-lifting belt, there are three basic types, each with specific pros and cons.

TRADITIONAL BELTS The traditional belts worn by many bodybuilders are made of leather and are wider in the back than in the front. They buckle like powerlifting belts, but are not as strong, providing less internal pressure. They should be considered midway between powerlifting belts and Velcro versions in terms of benefits.

POWERLIFTING BELTS These stiff, heavy-duty belts are the same width all the way around and buckle to adjust tightness. They are specifically designed for the sport of powerlifting—and not so much for safety. Nonetheless, a powerlifting belt's increased contact with the abdomen combined with its tightened, immovable buckle results in a surprising buildup of abdominal pressure. The heightened pressure leads to greater stability, which allows a wearer to lift heavier weights.

VELCRO BELTS These soft, flexible belts are usually made of synthetics. Because they fasten with hook-and-loop closures that can pop open, these are not as force-resistant as buckle belts, and they furnish less intra-abdominal pressure. They are useful for injury protection, but do not offer much of a performance boost.

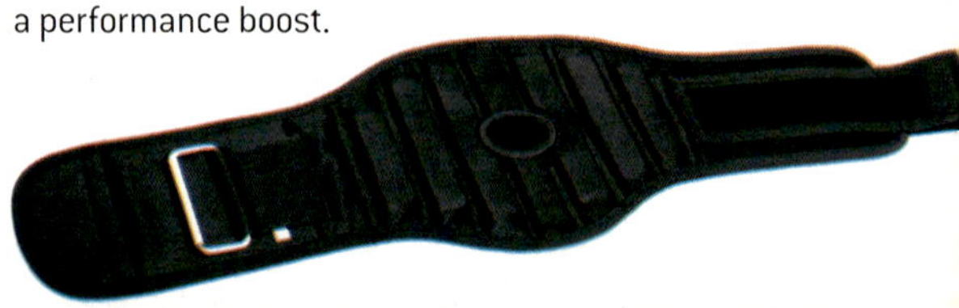

ACCELERATE YOUR RESULTS

Every experienced gym-goer understands that there are no true shortcuts, but sometimes certain methods can speed up results—at least enough that you don't become discouraged. The trick, as trainers say, is to work smarter instead of harder. Below are several examples of how to get greater results with less time spent on the floor. (And, as always, get your trainer's permission before attempting any intensive workouts.)

LIFT WITH A 2-4 TEMPO Remember that the speed with which you lift and lower weights is as much of a factor as how much you lift. For best results, follow a 2-4 count during resistance training—raise the weight (the concentric phase of an exercise) for a full two seconds, then take four seconds to return the weight to its starting position (the eccentric phase). According to research, exercisers who lower the weight in this slow, controlled manner gain nearly twice the strength as those who let gravity do the work.

INVESTIGATE INTERVAL TRAINING To get the most out of your gym time, don't just zone out on the same machinery set on the same moderate levels. Look into interval training—mixing periods of short, high-intensity exercise with longer, low-intensity exercise during the same workout. Many studies indicate that interval training boosts your calorie burn and improves overall fitness.

SUPERSIZE WITH SUPERSETS This is another proven way to increase weight-training results. Simply pick a muscle group, say the chest, and perform three or more different exercises for that group without resting in between. This blast of intensity should provide you with maximum results.

Ask the EXPERT

WHY DO SUPERSETS?

Supersets let you get in more work in less time and amp up the cardio benefits, increasing intensity levels, heart rate, and calories burned. This is especially true when supersetting large muscle groups like the chest and back, which places great oxygen demands on the body. You can superset within one body part or you can train two different ones. Effective combos include dumbbell incline chest presses and lat pull-downs, shoulder presses and pull-ups, and chest flies and reverse flies. Start with 5 to 8 reps, and work your way up to 10 or 12. Count three on the way down and two on the way up, and begin with lighter weights than you would normally use.

EXPLODE THAT PLATEAU

Explosive movement—those speed-driven exercises that require a strong burst of energy—is the antithesis of the slow, grinding resistance-training workouts many of us perform faithfully at the gym. Explosive training, which includes exercises like Olympic-style lifting, focuses on learning to move from muscle extension to a contraction in a rapid, or "explosive," manner.

Even though slow, controlled, steady weight training is the recommended way to break down muscle fibers, it can lead to plateaus in size and strength. Explosive movements, on the other hand, increase muscle fiber recruitment—how much your muscle is engaged during an activity. By increasing the number of fibers used, lifters can add more weight and affect more fibers—leading to greater changes in growth. Explosive movement can also furnish a welcome change of pace to your possibly stale routine of endless reps. Just remember that these movements should be performed early in your routine, if not right at the beginning.

MIX UP YOUR PUSH-UPS

From school gyms to military boot camps, the push-up is the go-to exercise. Sure, it builds great pecs, but it also does so much more—it's a powerful core-strengthener that builds power for daily activities and gets you in shape for other fitness pursuits.

This is also an exercise with seemingly endless variations that change up its effects. Balancing on a ball, for instance, forces you to fully engage your core. Switching leg or arm positions draws the focus from the pectorals to other muscles—bringing your hands together will engage those hard-to-tone triceps, while elevating your legs will get your delts working. And performing it on bent knees, rather than on your toes, is an easier modification perfect for fitness newbies.

Here is just a sampling of some of the many variations of the basic push-up.

A PUSH-UP

WHY Works all your major upper-body muscles
HOW Lie prone on the floor with your hands placed as wide or slightly wider than shoulder width, and then rise to a plank position. Lower your body, keeping it in a straight line from head to toe. Keeping your core engaged, exhale as you push back up to the plank position.

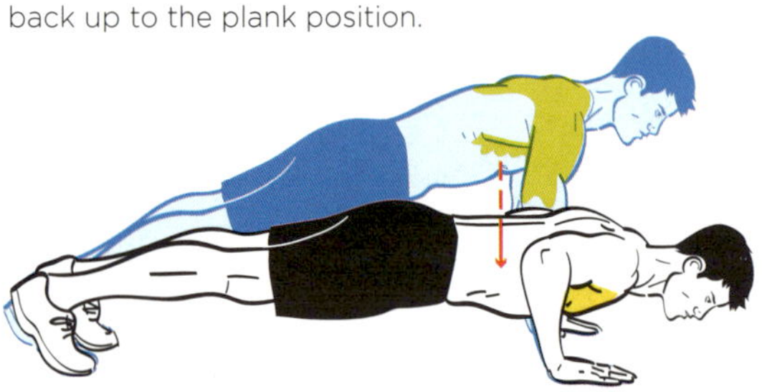

B BOSU BALL PUSH-UP

WHY Adds core, arm, and lower-body benefits
HOW Flip a BOSU® ball over onto its dome. Grip the sides or place your hands on top of it, and extend your legs straight behind you. Holding your body in a straight line, lower your chest to the ball, and then return to the starting position.

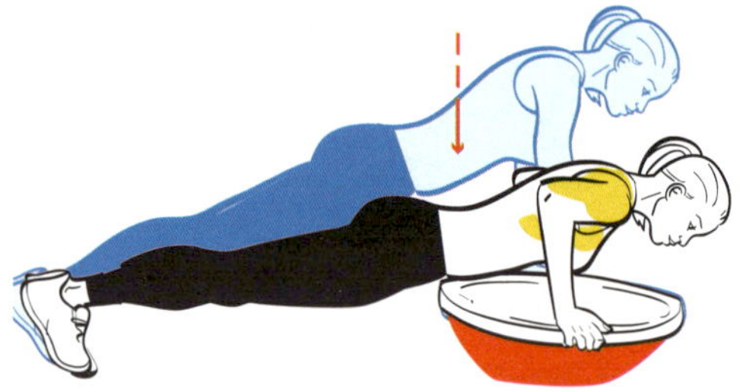

C DIAMOND PUSH-UP

WHY Changes the focus from pecs to triceps
HOW Place your hands on the floor in front of your chest with your fingers and thumbs pressed together to form a diamond shape. Extend your legs straight behind you. Lower your chest to the floor, and then press back into the starting position.

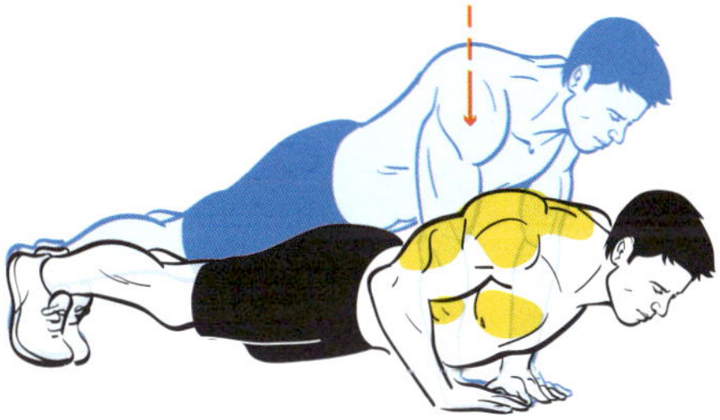

D DECLINE PUSH-UP

WHY Offers a greater challenge and more delts work
HOW Place your feet on a flat bench that is at least a foot off the ground or higher. From there, lower yourself into the regular push-up starting position. Keeping your forearms vertical, lower your chest to the ground, and then return to the starting position.

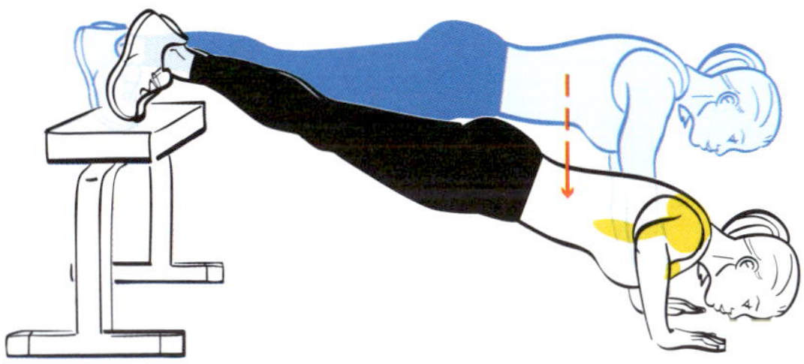

KNOW YOUR... BACK MUSCLES

Strong back muscles are essential—these muscles move the spine, hips, head, arms, and pelvis as you go about your daily life. This group includes the large latissimus dorsi muscles, the fan-shaped muscles located on the back of the torso that function to pull the arms down and back. Well-developed lats give bodybuilders their characteristic V-shaped torsos. The trapezius is the flat, triangular muscle that covers the back of the neck, shoulders, and thorax. The upper part of the trapezius elevates the shoulder and braces the shoulder girdle when you carry a weight. A bundle of muscles lying near the spine is known as the erector spinae. This critical group provides the resistance that allows you to control movements such as bending forward at the waist. Its extensor action then enables you to return your back to the erect position. Other major back muscles and groups are the teres major, rhomboideus, quadratus lumborum, and multifidus spinae.

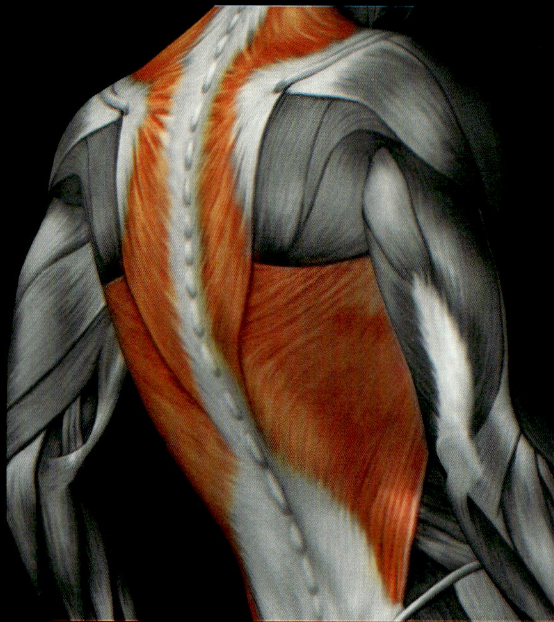

TOOLS of the TRADE

LEARN THE LAT PULL-DOWN

The lat pull-down machine is a great tool for beginners and intermediates to strengthen their back muscles in preparation for more taxing movements, like pull-ups and chin-ups. It also allows you to perfect your form for these strength moves while building up your back muscles, especially the latissimus dorsi.

One reason many people have difficulty with pull-ups and chin-ups—to the point where they cannot perform even one—is that they do not know how to engage their back muscles in the movement. The lat pull-down, which is a cable machine that supplies constant tension, acclimates you to using these muscles while focusing on proper posture. The overhand grip, especially, results in a weaker biceps reaction, forcing the body to use the back (lat) muscles.

Train on this machine three times a week, concentrating on proper form. Once reps become easier, start adding weight in small increments.

TARGETED workout

BUILD A BETTER BACK

The benefits of a strong back are twofold: a strong back keeps your spine aligned and pain-free; and toned back muscles shape your waist, making it look smaller and more defined. The key to strengthening the back is the appropriate gym equipment, because the back is the hardest body part to work without the right tools. Proper form is also essential, making far more difference than heavy weight.

To prevent back troubles, try performing this multi-target workout from a member of the Gold's Gym Fitness Institute, which allows you to adjust the weight and reps depending on your goal—strength or definition.

A **LAT PULL-DOWN MACHINE** This machine keeps the focus on your lats. You may sit or stand for this one. For strength, perform four sets of 6 to 10 reps; for definition, four sets of 12 to 15 reps.

HOW Grip the bar with your hands slightly wider than shoulder-width apart, arms straight up and palms facing forward. Pull the bar down to your chest, elbows out. Return slowly to the starting position, arms straight.

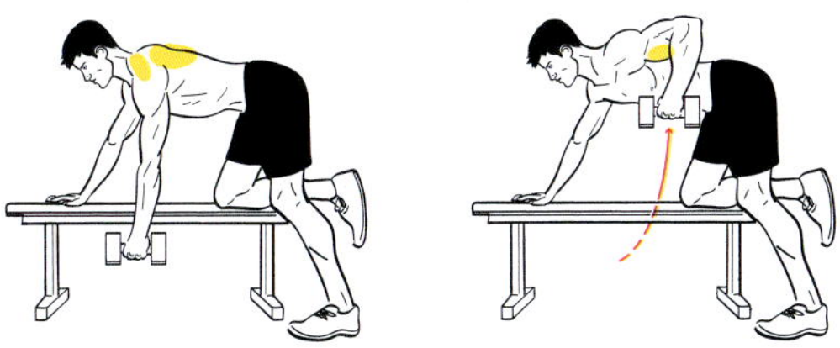

B **ONE-ARM DUMBBELL ROW** This row exercise works your back and arms, including your latissimus dorsi, rhomboids, middle trapezius, rear deltoids, and biceps. For strength, perform four sets of 6 to 10 reps with each arm; for definition, four sets of 12 to 15 reps.

HOW Grab a dumbbell in one hand, and put the opposite knee and hand on a bench so that your torso is parallel to the floor. Start with your arm extended straight down, and pull the dumbbell up to the side of your chest, keeping your arm close to your body. Lower to the starting position.

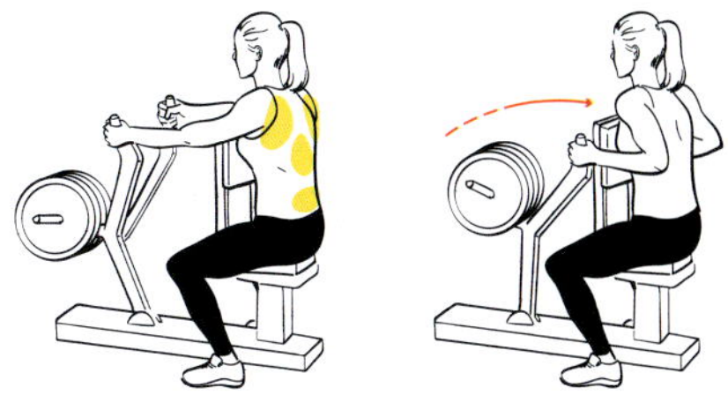

C **MACHINE ROW** The seated row machine is ideal for beginners who want to develop a strong, muscular back. For strength, perform four sets of 6 to 10 reps; for definition, four sets of 12 to 15 reps.

HOW Grab the handles of a seated row machine, and sit with your back straight, shoulder blades back. Pull the weight toward your body until the handles touch your abdomen. Return to the starting position.

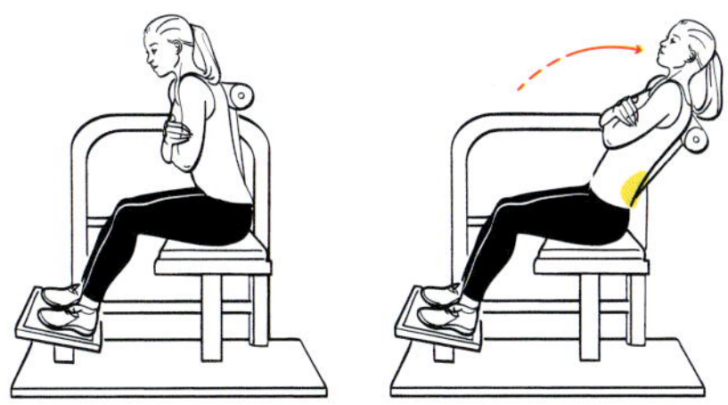

D **LOWER-BACK EXTENSION** Extensions stretch and strengthen your lower back. Perform them as a complement to crunches to develop a strong, balanced midsection. Complete four sets of 6 to 10 reps for strength only.

HOW Adjust the seat of a lower-back extension machine so that the axis is in line with your hips. Seat yourself with your upper back against the roller, and grasp the handles with your feet planted firmly on the footrest. Slowly push back until your spine is naturally erect. Maintain tension as you return to the starting position.

PULL YOURSELF UP

To build strength in the back and biceps, the pull-up tops the list of effective exercises. By using your own body weight for resistance, the pull-up works multiple muscle groups, including some of the big guns—rhomboids, biceps, mid and lower traps, obliques, and rectus abdominis—with an emphasis on the latissimus dorsi. Pull-ups not only build up the back, helping you avoid injuries to that vulnerable area, they improve stamina, create lean muscle mass, and strengthen your grip—a necessity for many competitive sports. Most gyms—and many urban playgrounds—feature a pull-up station. You can also purchase door- or wall-mounted bars for home pull-up workouts, if your multipurpose gym machine does not feature one of its own.

Pull-ups may look simple, but they can be a challenge to master; they are even sometimes used by the military in order to determine the fitness level of recruits. Try starting with only a few in the beginning, but hit the bar numerous times a day.

GET A GRIP

When performing pull-ups—and certain other exercises—there are three types of grips you will utilize. Each grip emphasizes different muscles: the overhand tends to primarily work the back; the underhand gets the biceps more involved. The placement of your hands on the bar also works different muscles. Positions include shoulder-width apart, slightly narrower than the shoulders, and slightly wider than the shoulders.

OVERHAND (PRONATED) GRIP Place your hands on the bar with palms facing away from you.

UNDERHAND (SUPINATED) GRIP Place your hands on the bar with palms facing toward you.

NEUTRAL GRIP Place your hands on the bar with palms facing each other. In this position, you perform the pull-up on a special apparatus with both crossbars and perpendicular bars.

KNOW THE DIFFERENCE

Closely related to the pull-up is the chin-up. "But aren't they the same thing?" you may ask. No, they are not—small, but crucial, differences in their execution means that they will train your muscles in slightly different ways. Although both exercises train the back and biceps, the chin-up places a bit more emphasis on the biceps. The chart below gives you a quick view of each move's major muscle focus, hand grip, leg position, and movement pattern.

EXERCISE	MAJOR FOCUS	HAND GRIP	LEG POSITION	MOVEMENT PATTERN
PULL-UP	latissimus dorsi	Use an overhand grip with hands just slightly wider than shoulder-width apart.	Bend your knees and cross your ankles.	You rely on shoulder adduction, meaning that your elbows come down and back from the sides.
CHIN-UP	latissimus dorsi/biceps brachii	Use an underhand grip with hands shoulder-width apart.	Let your legs hang straight down.	You rely on shoulder extension, meaning that your elbows come down and back from the front.

FINESSE THAT FIRST PULL-UP

Completing this movement correctly can become the Holy Grail of exercising for many people. For one thing, it requires really good technique—a combination of abdominal muscle control accompanied by powerful back muscles.

HOW Try starting with a dead hang, using an overhand grip with your hands shoulder-width apart. Then lean back so that your chest is pointed toward the bar. Keep your shoulder blades pinched together, and keep your forearms as vertical as you can. Initiate the pull by exhaling forcefully, retracting your shoulders down and back with your lats and using your biceps to flex your elbows. Your aim is to raise your chest, not the tops of your shoulders, to meet the bar. A perfect pull-up tops out with your chin rising just above the bar, and ends with steady inhalations as you slowly lower until your shoulders are at your ears and your elbows are locked straight. Anything less—cheating on either end—will keep you from getting stronger.

MIX IT UP

If at first you find you can't perform even one pull-up, there are several ways to increase your upper-body strength before giving it another shot. Try easier, assisted versions—like the band-assisted chin-up—and then move on to simple pull-ups. After mastering those, try the more challenging variations.

BAND-ASSISTED CHIN-UP Loop a resistance band over the bar, and place one foot in the loop. Use an underhand grip with your hands shoulder-width apart. Engage your abs, and then bend your elbows to pull your body up until your chin is above bar. Slowly lower back down.

BASIC CHIN-UP Use an underhand (supinated) grip with your hands placed shoulder-width apart or slightly narrower. The focus shifts to the biceps a bit more than with a pull-up.

CLOSE-GRIP PULL-UP Use an overhand grip with your hands nearly touching. The focus includes your lats, serratus anterior, and humeral muscles.

WIDE-GRIP PULL-UP Use an overhand grip with your hands placed a few inches beyond shoulder-width apart. This keeps the focus on your lats.

MIXED GRIP PULL-UP Place one hand in the overhand position and the other in the underhand position. This changes the way each arm utilizes your elbow flexor muscles.

WEIGHTED PULL-UP Add further resistance by using a dipping belt with a weight plate, grasping a dumbbell or other weight with your feet, or wearing a weighted vest or shorts.

KNOW YOUR ROW

An old-school favorite of powerlifters and bodybuilders, the barbell row (a.k.a. bent-over barbell row) is a pull-type compound exercise that is used to strengthen a variety of back muscles, as well as the hips and arms. It is an anti-flexion exercise—meaning that you use your lower-back muscles to keep your torso from folding over—so it builds lower-back strength and stability, which will help you improve your posture. As with any exercise, proper form makes all the difference.

A **BENT-OVER BARBELL ROW** Mastering this basic row will help strengthen your back, especially your lats and traps.

HOW Holding a barbell, stand with your toes pointing slightly outward. Keeping your lower back straight, bend your knees slightly, and hinge forward at the hips. Lead with your elbows, pulling them toward the ceiling until the bar reaches the level of your upper waist. Return the bar to the floor, so that your arms are fully extended and your shoulders are stretched downward.

B **BENT-OVER TWO-ARM LONG BARBELL ROW** This row targets the lower and middle back, the lats, and the biceps.

HOW Use an Olympic bar with weight plates on one end only. Put the other end of the bar against a wall or something heavy so it can't slide backwards. Straddle the bar with your knees slightly bent, and bend forward at the waist. Grasp the bar with a neutral grip, your palms facing each other, and pull the bar toward your abdomen. Return to the starting position.

C **UPRIGHT BARBELL ROW** The upright row moves the target upward to the trapezius muscles of your upper back, neck, and shoulders and also works the deltoids and biceps. The narrower the grip, the greater the emphasis on the traps.

HOW Stand upright grasping a barbell with a shoulder-width or slightly narrower overhand grip. With your elbows leading, pull the bar upward to neck height and allow your wrists to flex as you lift the bar. Lower the bar to the starting position.

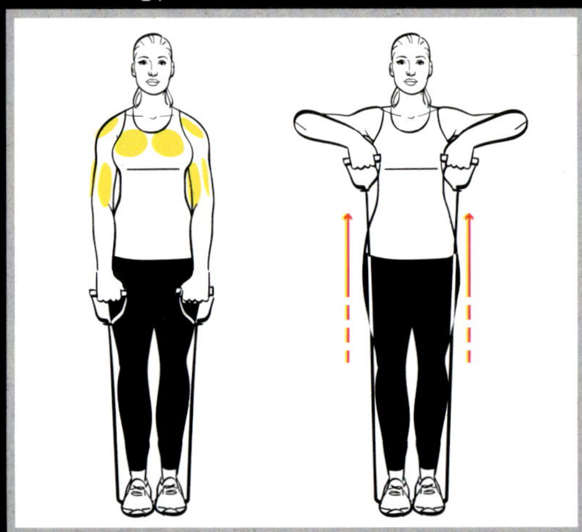

D **RESISTANCE BAND UPRIGHT ROW** Like the barbell version, the resistance-band version emphasizes the trapezius. Because you only need to pack a simple band, it's a great move for those travelers who want to stay in shape on the road without overloading their luggage with heavy weights.

HOW Stand with your feet positioned over the center of a resistance band, and grip each handle with your palms facing the front of your thighs. With your elbows leading, pull the band straight up the front of your body to chest or shoulder height to form a wide V with your elbows. Lower the handles to the starting position.

SHOW RESPECT

GYM etiquette

Always treat the gym's equipment with respect; this is especially important when you are working with barbells and dumbbells. Remember that these are heavy, solid objects, and all it can take is a split second of careless behavior for an injury to occur. So always use respect when handling weights: never swing dumbbells, barbells, or plate weights when there are others nearby, and never toss them onto the floor following a set. When you finish working with weights, re-rack the plates, barbells, and dumbbells for others to use.

SAY HELLO TO MR. SMITH

TOOLS of the TRADE

The Smith machine, which is used in weight training, consists of a stabilized framework with a movable weight bar that is fixed within two steel tracks. This restricts the weight to vertical or near vertical movement. You can use a Smith machine for a variety of exercises, including bench presses, shoulder presses, and squats. Because the barbell can be secured in any horizontal position with a simple twist of the bar, it is safer for beginners or lifters without spotters. The contained barbell also requires less core stabilization by the lifter, so most individuals can handle more weight on the Smith.

A similar piece of equipment is the power cage (also called a power rack, squat cage, or squat rack), which features four vertical posts with two movable horizontal bar catchers on each side. Many power cages also include pull-up bars. A power cage will allow for a barbell workout without the movement restrictions imposed by the Smith machine.

SWIM LIKE SUPERMAN . . . OR GO TO THE DOGS

Nothing else can sideline you from your workout routine—or even just your daily activities—like lower-back pain. And for good reason: the lumbar region of your spine supports the majority of your body. And an overwhelming majority of us will suffer from a back injury sometime in our lives, most often of the lower back. Inactivity is also a culprit, with those long hours sitting at a desk taking a toll on your spine.

Strengthening the muscles that support your spine is therefore essential. You don't need to be Superman (or Superwoman), but taking a few cues from his midair form is a great way to start a lower-back strengthening routine. Adding in the bird dog exercise will keep your back from going to the dogs.

A BIRD DOG

WHY The bird dog primarily targets the erector spinae muscles, which run along your spine and are responsible for extending your torso. This exercise, also called the quadruped arm/leg raise, uses your body weight as resistance to strengthen your lower back.

HOW Start on your hands and knees, with your back straight and abs pulled in. Keep your torso stable and your abs engaged as you contract one of your arms and the opposite leg into your body. Extend that arm outward along with the leg. Hold for up to 15 seconds. Return to the starting position, switch sides, and repeat.

B SWIMMING SUPERMAN

WHY Also known as land swimming, this exercise combines a stationary Superman exercise with the movements of swimming so that you strengthen your back, core, and leg muscles. Swimming exercises also help improve coordination, thus getting you to move your arms and legs independently from the torso, which should remain solid and stable.

HOW Lie face-down on the floor with your neck parallel to the floor. Lift your right hand and left leg off the floor simultaneously. Repeat with the left hand and right leg, and then continue switching back and forth as if you were swimming on land, making sure to fully engage your back and butt muscles.

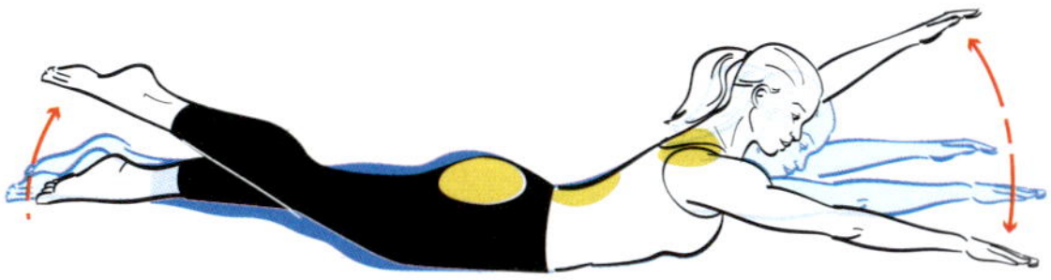

C STABILITY BALL SUPERMAN

WHY A Superman performed on a stability ball is a smart choice if you are trying to prevent back pain. Any Superman strengthens your back and core, and adding in the ball forces you to use muscles that are often inhibited as you sit at a desk all day, including the glutes, scapular rotators, and posterior deltoids.

HOW Balance on a stability ball with your stomach on top and your toes on the floor. Let your torso fall over the ball, and relax your arms by your sides. Starting with your head and upper back, slowly lift your spine until it's straight. Slowly return to the start.

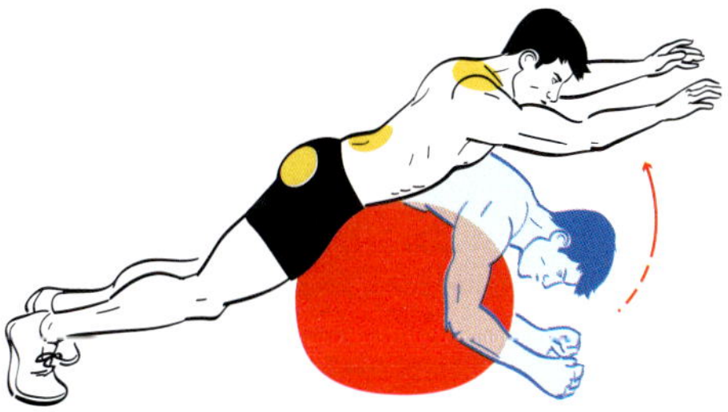

KNOW YOUR... DELTOIDS

With the greatest range of motion of any joint in the human body, your shoulder needs strong muscles to support it. The deltoids, the largest and strongest of the shoulder muscles, are up to that challenge. Divided into the front, middle, and rear sections called the deltoideus anterior, medialis, and posterior, the delts (as they are known in gym circles) form the outer layer of shoulder muscle. They work to elevate and rotate the arm. The trapezius, located on the back, also works to enable shoulder movement, moving, rotating, and stabilizing the scapula (shoulder blade), while the rhomboid muscle is chiefly responsible for its retraction. Also working the scapula is the serratus anterior, located along your side. This muscle is known as the boxer's muscle because it is largely responsible for the movement that occurs when you throw a punch.

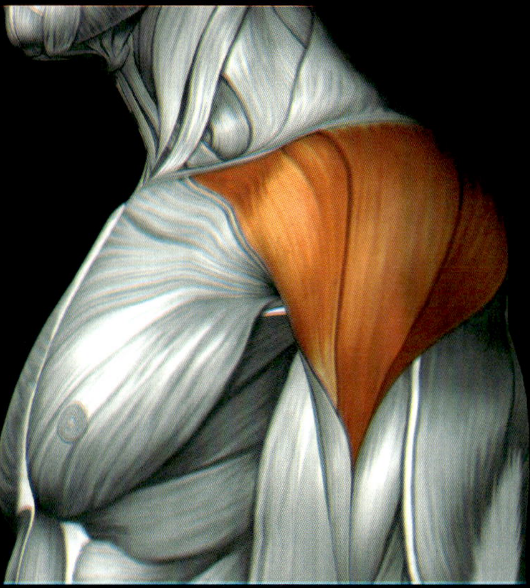

PROTECT YOUR SHOULDERS

The rotator cuff is a group of tendons and muscles in the shoulder that connect the upper arm to the shoulder blade. The rotator cuff tendons provide stability to the shoulder, and the muscles allow the shoulder to rotate.

ROTATOR CUFF If you're having trouble reaching during your workout, it may not be the time to work through the pain; it may be a rotator cuff injury. Other signs are tenderness during a military press or when lifting weight away from your body.

WHAT TO DO Avoid lifts that involve raising your hands above your head and shoulders, and work to strengthen the four muscles of the rotator cuff—the supraspinatus, infraspinatus, teres minor, and subscapularis. This is done often through internal and external rotation exercises. For internal rotation, keep your upper arm close to your side with your elbow bent 90 degrees, then bring the hand across your body, as if you were shutting a door. Then, for external rotation, bring your hand in the opposite direction, away from the middle of your body.

TARGETED workout

SHOULDER THE WEIGHT

This strengthening workout from the experts at the Gold's Gym Fitness Institute targets all three major shoulder muscles, especially the anterior and posterior delts, which will help you to fight off the effects of cubicle crunch. Along with counteracting the consequences of slouching, it tones and defines your upper body and traps. If you're a beginner, start off with a pair of five-pound (2.3 kg) dumbbells.

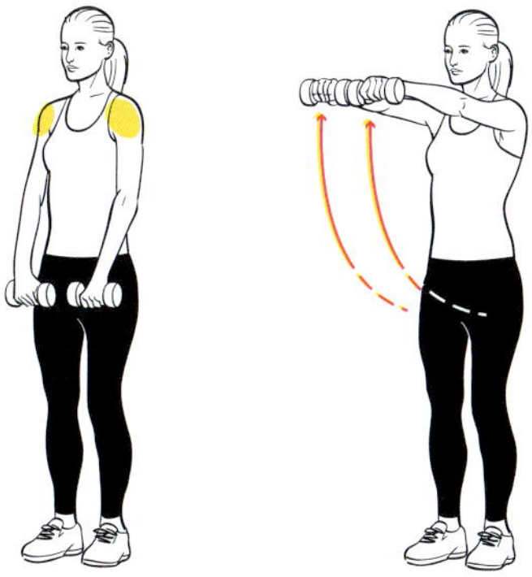

A **DUMBBELL FRONT RAISE** This exercise is an effective move to isolate your anterior deltoid muscles. Perform four sets of 12 reps.

HOW Standing, hold dumbbells in front of you with your palms facing your legs. Keep your elbows and knees slightly bent as you raise your arms straight in front of you to shoulder level. Slowly return to the starting position.

B **REVERSE FLY** This exercise targets your posterior deltoids, along with the rhomboid and middle trapezius muscles of your upper back. Perform four sets of 12 reps.

HOW Standing, hold dumbbells with your palms facing each other. Bend your torso forward, so that it forms a 45-degree angle with the floor. With elbows slightly bent, raise the dumbbells up and out to the sides until they are parallel to the floor. As you lift the weights, focus on squeezing your shoulder blades together.

C **DUMBBELL LATERAL RAISE** Lifting laterally activates your posterior deltoids and upper-back muscles. Perform four sets of 12 reps.

HOW Standing, hold dumbbells with your palms facing each other. Keeping your elbows and knees slightly bent, raise your arms out from your sides in wide arcs to about shoulder level. Slowly return to the starting position.

D **SEATED MILITARY PRESS** While building anterior deltoid strength, this exercise also targets the upper back. Perform four sets of 12 reps.

HOW Sit holding a dumbbell in each hand, and raise them to shoulder level with palms facing out and elbows bent. Press the weights up and toward each other as you straighten your arms, keeping a slight bend in your elbows at the top. Slowly bring down the weights, and return to the starting position.

KNOW YOUR... BICEPS

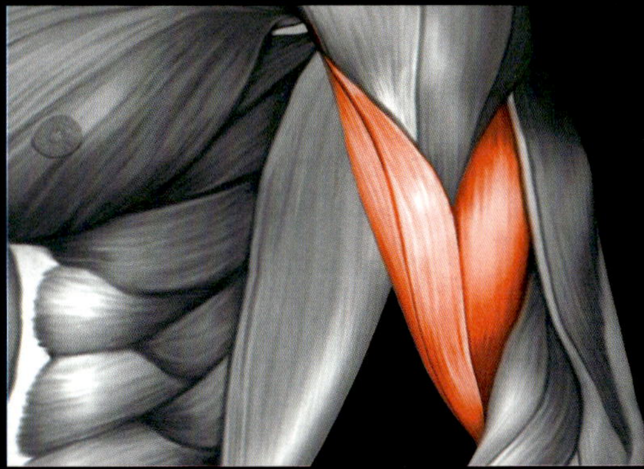

Of the diverse and numerous muscles of the arm, the biceps brachii is often the main focus of those who want to get in shape—or show off their great "guns." The biceps, located on the upper arms, consists of two bundles of muscles or "heads." It is a flexor muscle that bends the elbow to bring your lower arm toward the upper arm, and it also acts to turn your palm upward. Because the biceps also crosses your shoulder joint, it helps bring your arm forward and upward or across your body.

TOOLS of the TRADE

DO IT WITH DUMBBELLS

One of the most utilized pieces of weight-training equipment, a dumbbell is a free weight, typically held in the hand, that can be used singly or in pairs. Like smaller versions of barbells, adjustable dumbbells have weight plates that can be changed; other types use fixed weights. They vary in weight from a few pounds or kilos to more than a hundred and can be made from iron, chrome, or other materials, and the weight plates can be round or hexagonal shaped (which prevents them from rolling when you place them on the floor). There are three main categories.

FIXED-WEIGHT Commercial gyms use high-end, fixed-weight dumbbells generally made from bars with securely welded iron plates. The basic fixed-weight dumbbells for home use, however, are weights formed into in a classic dumbbell shape. These kinds of dumbbells are usually the most inexpensive choice, and are often cast iron coated with rubber or neoprene for comfort, or are a rigid plastic shell filled with concrete. Look for sets like the Gold's Gym Dumbbell Set that features color-coded pairs of neoprene weights of 3 pounds (1.36 kg), 5 pounds (2.27 kg), and 8 pounds (3.83 kg).

ADJUSTABLE For space-conscious home exercisers, adjustable dumbbells are a better choice than fixed-weight because they give you a variety of weight levels with a single dumbbell. Adjustable dumbbells consist of a metal bar (which are often knurled, or cross-hatched, to improve grip), upon which you slide disks that are secured with clips or collars. Gold's Gym offers the Transformer Dumbbell set with a Click and Slide System that easily adjusts the weight from 9.9 pounds (4.5 kg) to 44 pounds (20 kg).

SELECTORIZED These dumbbells take adjustable dumbbells a step further, allowing you to easily change the number of plates while the dumbbell is resting in a stand.

LEARN TO CURL

BEST EXERCISES

The curl is probably the best-known exercise for the biceps. And the basic curl is one of the easiest resistance-training moves to understand (press up, lower down)—yet getting the form right takes a lot of practice.

Here are four of the many variations of this classic—think about incorporating one or more of them into your workout.

RACK 'EM UP

GYM *etiquette*

Always place your dumbbells in their racks after you're done exercising. It's poor gym etiquette to leave plates loaded on a leg press at the end of your sets or to leave barbells or dumbbells lying on the floor where someone could trip over them. If you're able to lift weights during an exercise, then you're able to re-rack them when you're done. Consideration and courtesy keep things moving smoothly in the gym.

A **STANDING BICEPS CURL** Learning the proper form for the basic biceps curl is essential, helping you to tone your upper-arm muscles and also preparing you for trickier curl variations. As with most curls, you can perform the basic curls seated or standing. Just be sure to pick the appropriate amount of weight for your fitness level—you'll get more out of well-performed reps at a light weight than you will from sloppily performed reps with more impressive poundage.

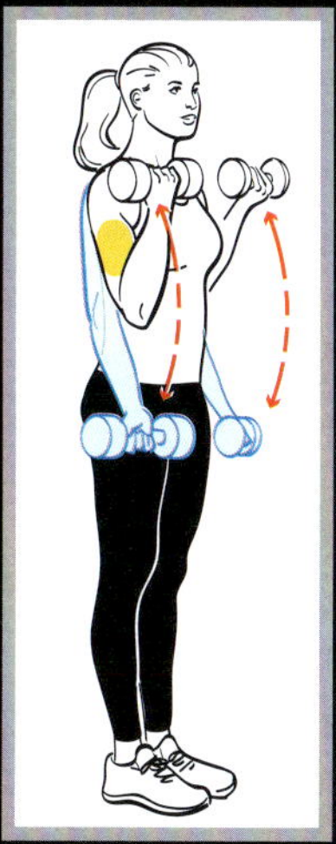

HOW Grab a pair of dumbbells, and let them hang at arm's length. Turn your arms so that your palms face forward. Without moving your upper arms, bend your elbows, and curl the dumbbells upward until they are close to your shoulders. Pause, then slowly lower back to the starting position. Each time you return to the starting position, completely straighten your arms.

B **CONCENTRATION CURL** The concentration curl offers a great biceps workout that stimulates the muscle fibers on the peak of the biceps. Taking a seated position limits the degree momentum plays in the execution of the curl, which keeps the focus on where it should be: right on that biceps muscle.

HOW Sit at the edge of a flat bench holding a dumbbell with your left arm. Place the back of your upper arm on top of your inner left thigh, and rotate your palm until it is facing away from your thigh. Holding your upper arm stationary, curl the weight upward while contracting your biceps until the dumbbell is at shoulder level. Squeeze your biceps, and hold the contracted position for a second. Slowly begin to bring the dumbbell back to a starting position. Perform the desired reps, and then repeat with the right arm.

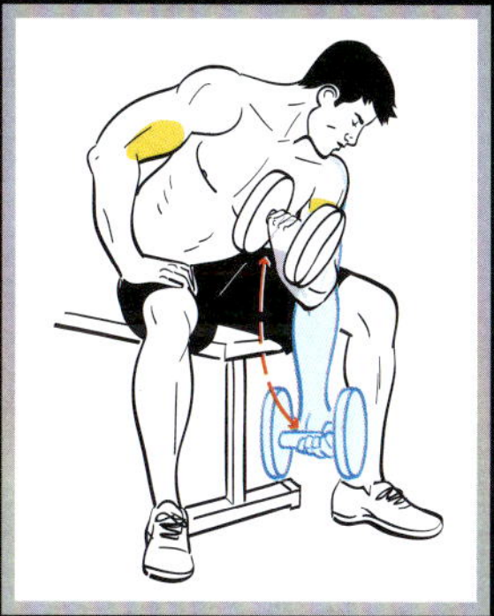

C **EZ BAR PREACHER CURL** The EZ bar is a speciality barbell with a curved bar that allows you to grasp it with your palms in a more natural, less supinated (upward) position. In the EZ bar preacher curl, resting your arms on the sloping pad of a preacher bench will isolate your biceps and force them to work without the help of other upper-body muscles.

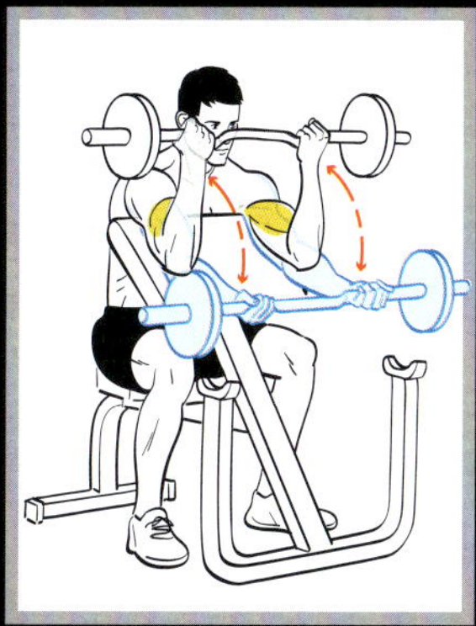

HOW Grab an EZ bar with your hands in the curved sections. Rest your upper arms on the sloping pad of a preacher bench, and hold the bar in front of you with your elbows slightly bent. Without moving your upper arms, bend your elbows, and curl the bar toward your shoulders. Pause, then slowly lower the weight back to the starting position.

D **HAMMER CURL** The hammer curl is all about the angles—flipping your basic curl grip to its side. This small change in your grip transfers morof the work from your biceps brachii to your brachialis—a muscle that can make your arms look thicker.

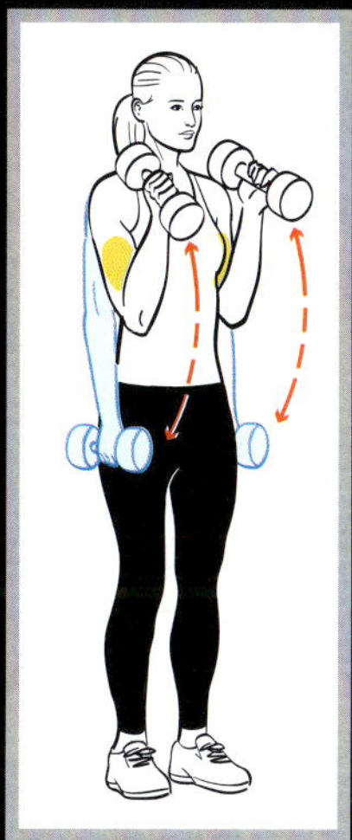

HOW Grab a pair of dumbbells, and let them hang at arm's length next to your sides with your palms facing your thighs. Keeping your upper arms still, bend your elbows, and curl the dumbbells as close to your shoulders as you can. Maintain the contracted position for a second, and then slowly lower the weight back to the starting position. Make sure to completely straighten your arms each time you return to the starting position.

KNOW YOUR... TRICEPS

The triceps brachii is a three-headed extensor muscle located on the back of the upper arm. It is the extensor muscle of your elbow joint, and it also fixates your elbow when you use your forearm and hand for fine movements, such as writing. Its long head comes into play when you need to generate sustained force; the medial head enables more precise, low-force movements; and the lateral head allows for movements requiring occasional high-intensity force. The triceps is the antagonist of the biceps. With antagonistic pairs, one muscle contracts as the other relaxes—in this case, the triceps relaxes while the biceps contracts to lift the arm.

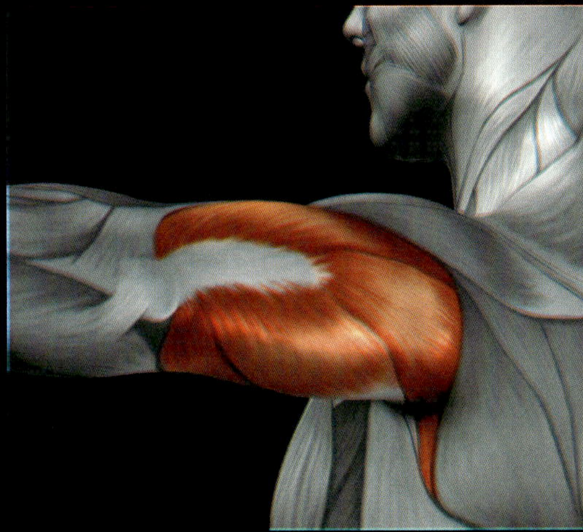

TIGHTEN UP THOSE TRICEPS

As most gym-goers know, certain parts of the body stubbornly resist toning and conditioning. Perhaps the most notorious of these are the triceps, the muscles located at the back of your arms. They are not only a tricky spot to create definition, they can become saggy, especially after a period of weight loss.

Unfortunately, we often ignore our triceps. One possible reason is that we tend to "only work the muscles we see"—that is, we can't view our triceps with the same clarity that we see our abs, biceps, and chest and so don't give them priority. Furthermore, these muscles require deliberate movement to exercise them, making them difficult to work effectively. Weight training is the answer to taming those triceps, using either free weights or weight machines. Conditioning them is also important because any time there is a deficiency in one muscle group—in this case the triceps—other muscles—like the biceps—have to work harder, tiring you out more quickly. So include a triceps exercise in your weekly routine, and before long you'll notice sleek, lean underarms taking shape.

THINK *about it*

There was a time when many gym-goers focused only on building "show" muscles, but the current approach is to aim for long, lean, functionally strong muscles. That's the new sexy.

TARGETED workout

TONE AND DEFINE YOUR TRICEPS

The key to sleek-looking arms is a targeted triceps routine. These four exercises utilize weights—dumbbells, barbells, and cable machine—to work all three heads of the triceps, preparing them for the next level of training. To allow for adequate recovery, perform this workout once a week only. Start with one set of each, and work your way up to four.

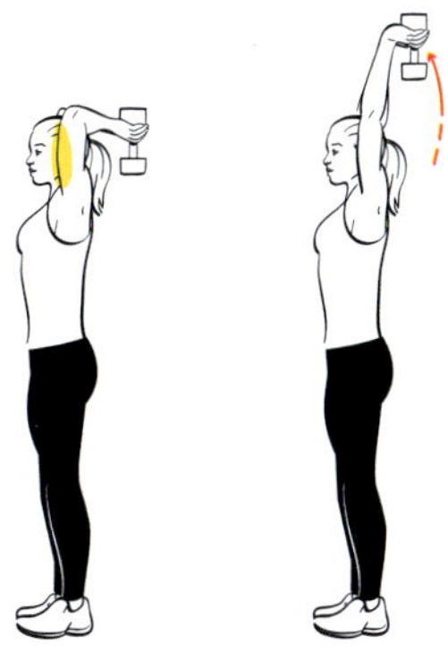

A **OVERHEAD TRICEPS EXTENSION** To keep the focus on your triceps, keep your shoulders down and your elbows as close to your ears as possible, and avoid arching your back. Perform one to four sets of 12 reps.

HOW Stand with your knees soft and your arms straight up with your elbows next to ears, holding a dumbbell with both hands. Bend your elbows to a 90-degree angle. Squeeze your triceps to straighten your arms, pressing the dumbbell up. Slowly lower back to the starting position.

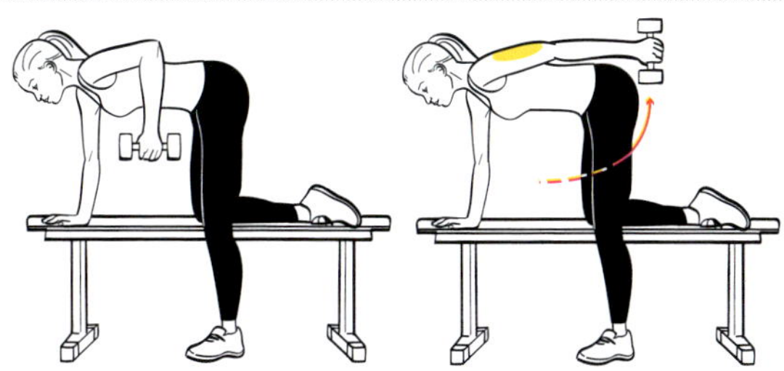

B **ONE-ARM KICKBACK** To perfect your form, be sure not to lock your elbow at the top of the movement. Straighten your arm, but keep your elbow slightly bent. Perform one to four sets of 12 reps with each arm.

HOW Holding a dumbbell in your left hand, place your right knee on a flat bench, and bend forward, bracing yourself with your palm. Bend your right elbow to a 90-degree angle, and then slowly straighten your arm. Hold for a moment, and then return to the starting position.

C **BARBELL SKULL CRUSHER** Be sure to recruit a spotter for this exercise—its name is a reminder of what can happen if you do the exercise improperly and drop the barbell. Perform one to four sets of 10 reps.

HOW Lie face-up on a bench, and extend both arms overhead, grasping barbell with an overhand grip. Bend your elbows so that your forearms are parallel to the floor. Slowly straighten your arms, and then lower to the starting position.

D **CABLE ROPE OVERHEAD EXTENSION** If you are performing this exercise properly, you'll feel a distinct stretch in your triceps. Perform one to four sets of 12 reps.

HOW Stand with your feet shoulder-width apart, and keep your back straight and abs tightly drawn in. Grab the ends of a cable rope with both hands with your palms facing up, and then raise the rope over your head. Once your arms are fully extended, slowly lower the rope in an arc behind your head. Hold for a count, then slowly raise the rope back to the start.

KNOW YOUR... ABDOMINALS

The main abdominal muscle, the rectus abdominis, is a paired muscle running vertically along your abdomen, beginning at the pubic bone and ending at the sternum. The abs work to contract your body forward and are important postural and core muscles. A targeted abdominal workout, paired with a proper diet, results in the highly defined look known as "six-pack" or "washboard" abs.

Along with the rectus abdominis is the transversus abdominis, a deep muscle in the abdominal wall lying beneath the internal oblique muscle. Nicknamed the corset muscle, a well-toned transversus abdominis works to pull in your abdomen, preventing it from protruding. The external obliques, the side abdominals, are located on each side of the rectus abdominis, and lying beneath the external obliques are the internal obliques. This muscle group flexes the rib cage and the pelvic bones together, bends the torso sideways, and rotates the torso.

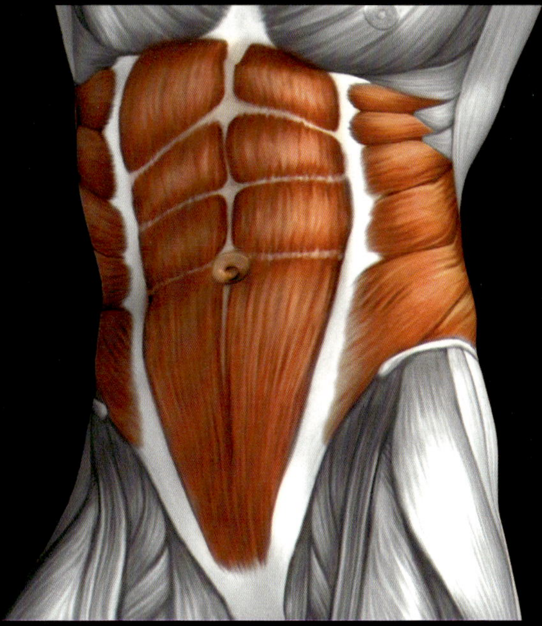

RIP YOUR ABS

In recent years, a spate of ultra-fit Hollywood hunks—and hunkettes—popularized the look of extremely defined abdominal muscles, the infamous "six pack." This sculpted appearance is not achieved without concentrated effort, but it can be worth all the hard work, especially if you spend a lot of time at the beach or poolside.

To trim your midsection, you must watch your nutrition. Try to eat the proper amounts of protein and healthy fats, and remember your post-workout complex carbs. At the gym, forget doing thousands of crunches and add in core-centric exercises, such as the captain's chair knee raise that employs more than twice the abdominal activity of basic crunches. Be sure to include exercises that work your obliques—those side abs that are too often hidden behind fat deposits (those pesky love handles).

High-intensity, whole-body resistance training will also promote post-exercise fat burning. Try to maintain proper sleep habits, and keep stress levels low to avoid hormonal changes that affect waist size. This is one reason many women have trouble getting ripped—their hormonal makeup contains less testosterone, making it more difficult to build muscle mass and burn calories during and after exercise.

Result may vary, but most individuals will start to see results in 12 weeks. Finally, don't think that all you need is a fat-burning supplement. There are no shortcuts to ripped abs.

SALUTE THE CAPTAIN

If you are serious about strengthening your abs, try the captain's chair knee raise. In recent studies, this exercise stimulated 210 percent more ab activity in the study's participants than the traditional crunch. It also engages the hard-to-work lower abs.

HOW Stand on the captain's chair machine or power tower. Grip the handles, and press your back against the pad. Keeping your feet close together, remove them from the support steps so that your legs dangle freely. Engage your abs, and bring your knees up toward your chest, keeping your upper back and shoulders strong. Then, with slow, controlled movements, lower your legs back to the starting position.

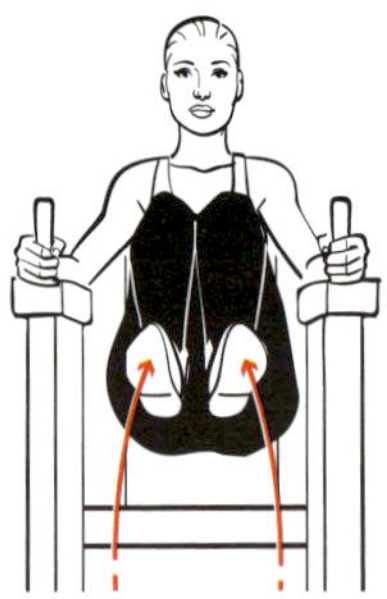

TARGETED workout

WHITTLE YOUR WAIST

Choosing a workout to tone your midsection means including exercises that target the obliques, the muscles that define and shape your waist.

Just about any move that calls for you to reach to the side will work these muscles, but ones that also incorporate your rectus and transversus abdominis will more effectively sculpt and slim your waistline. Exercises that target the obliques and the intercostals—several additional groups of muscles that run between the ribs—also help to get you in top shape for rotational sports like tennis and golf.

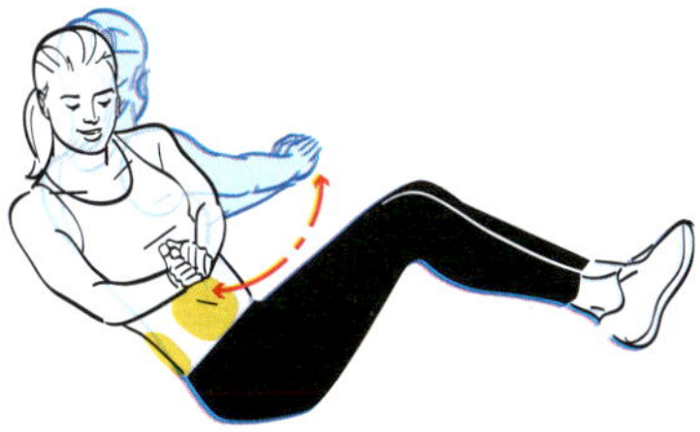

A **SEATED RUSSIAN TWIST** This ab exercise really works your obliques, while also engaging your back muscles. Perform three sets of 10 reps.

HOW Sit on the floor with your knees bent, pull your abs to your spine, and lean back a few inches while lifting your feet off the floor. Keep your back straight, reach your arms out in front of you, and twist your torso to the right, then to the left.

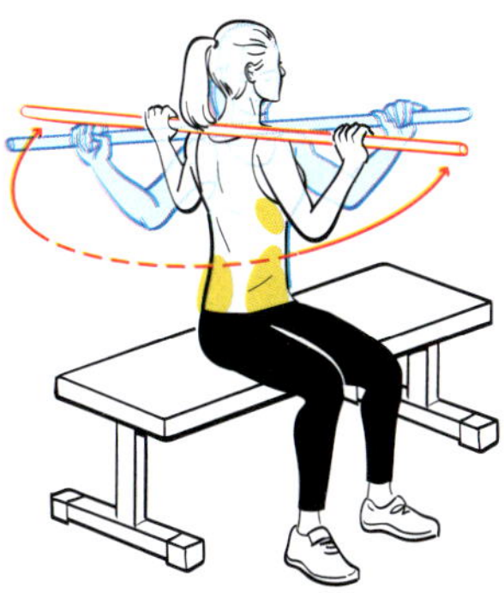

B **BROOM TWIST** This twist is a great abdominal exercise for increasing flexibility and working out your obliques. Perform three sets of 10 reps.

HOW Place a broomstick across the back of your shoulders, holding it with an overhand grip with your hands, and sit with your back straight, abs tight, and chin up. Twist your upper body to one side, and then slowly twist to the other side. Continue without stopping for the full number of reps.

C **CABLE WOOD CHOP** The wood-chop motion engages your obliques, back, shoulders, and legs. Repeat on the opposite side for a total of two sets of 10 reps on each side.

HOW Stand sideways to a cable stack with a D-handle set low. Squat, and hold it with both hands, arms extended toward the anchor point. Extend your legs, and twist through your waist to bring the handle above your opposite shoulder. Return to the start, following the same path of motion.

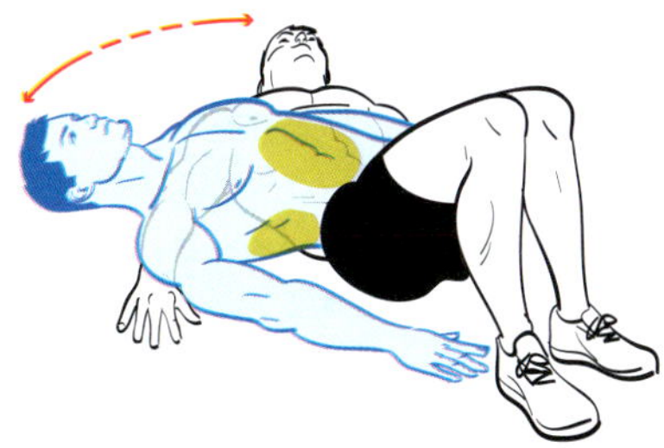

D **PENGUIN CRUNCH** This reaching exercise uses extension and lateral movement to target your abs and obliques. Complete three sets of 10 reps.

HOW Lie on your back with your knees bent and feet flat, hip-width apart, and arms at your sides. Crunch, and slightly lift your upper body, and then rotate your torso to one side, trying to touch your fingertips to your heel by sliding your hand across the floor. Then rotate to the other side with your other hand. Continue alternating fingertip-to-heel touches.

THINK *about it*

To make the penguin crunch a little more challenging, just move your heels farther away from your body, so you extend more in order to touch them. To make it easier, scoot them in closer.

CUSTOMIZE YOUR CRUNCH

When you think of exercises for the abs, what's the first one that comes to mind? Yeah ... it's the crunch. A basic crunch is simple in theory, but not always easy to execute properly in reality. Form is everything, especially if you have lower-back or neck problems.

PULL IN YOUR ABS Keep your abs pulled in. This places greater tension on them, so that you don't overarch your lower back.

DON'T PULL ON YOUR NECK Don't pull on your neck with your hands or draw your elbows in, as it may strain your neck muscles and vertebrae.

CURL AND LIFT Curl forward as if doubling over, as well as lift your torso and shoulders. Don't just yank your head, neck, and shoulder blades off the floor.

KEEP IT SMALL The crunch is a small movement. No need to touch your head to your knees—lifting just a few inches off the floor is high enough to effectively engage your abdominal muscles.

Once you've mastered the basic moves, try the variations below that amp up the basic crunch to really maximize your abs workout.

A BASIC CRUNCH

WHY Strengthens the abdominals.

HOW Lie down on your back with your knees bent and feet flat on the floor, hip-width apart. Cross your hands over your chest or bring them together behind your head. Keeping your neck relaxed, roll your upper back off the floor so that your head, neck, and shoulder blades lift off the floor. Hold for a moment at the top, and then lower slowly.

B REVERSE CRUNCH

WHY This exercise has been shown to stimulate more than twice as much abdominal activity than the traditional basic crunch.

HOW Lie on your back, and extend your arms at your sides. Raise your knees and feet so that they create a 90-degree angle. Contract your abs, and exhale as you lift your hips off the floor; your knees will move toward your head. Inhale, and slowly lower.

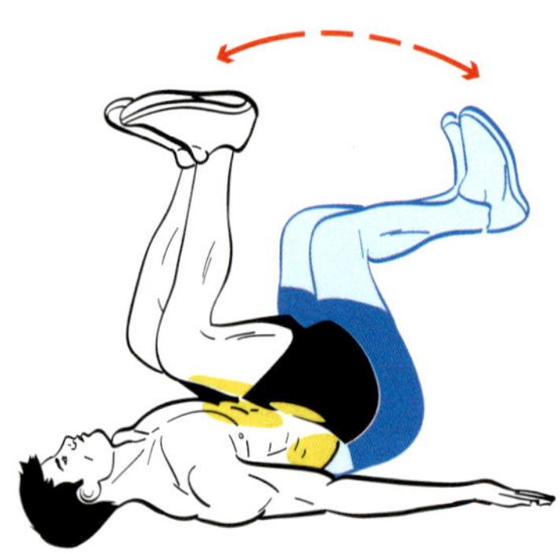

C BICYCLE CRUNCH

WHY One rep reaps the benefits of many crunches.

HOW Lie on your back. Put your hands behind your head. Lift your legs off the floor, and then extend your right leg while bringing your left knee up toward your chest. Lift your head, neck and shoulders up and reach with your right elbow across your body toward your left knee. Lower back down. Keep alternating sides in a pedaling motion.

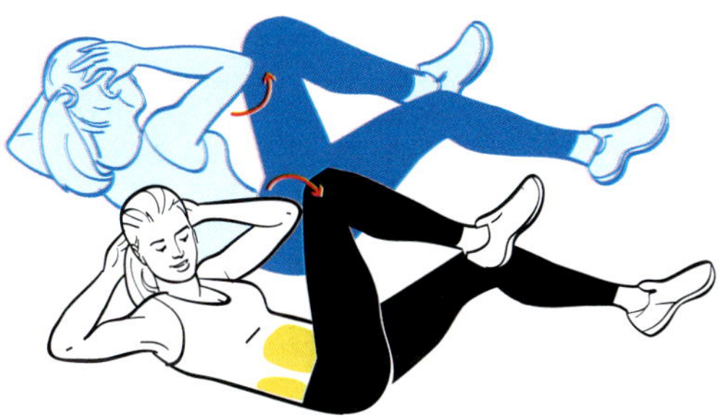

D DOUBLE CRUNCH

WHY Combines the moves of a basic crunch with the power of a reverse crunch that will target your lower abdominals.

HOW Lie on your back with your legs bent, hands behind your head and feet flat on the floor. While exhaling, contract your abs and simultaneously raise your head and torso with your hips and knees, bringing them toward each other to touch.

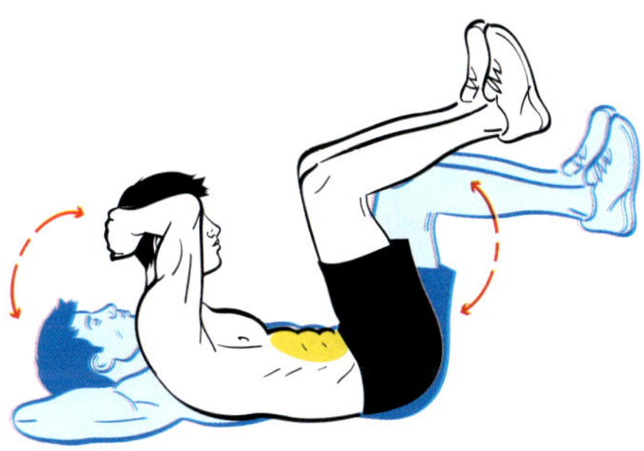

KNOW YOUR... QUADRICEPS

Among the strongest muscles in your body, the four-headed quadriceps femoris covers just about all of your femur—the long bone of your thigh. The quadriceps femoris actually includes four front thigh muscles—the rectus femoris vastus lateralis, vastus medialis, and vastus intermedius. This group functions to extend your leg. The rectus femoris attaches to the ilium bone of the pelvis, so it also flexes the hip—an action essential to walking or running as it swings the leg forward into the next step you take. The vastus medialis, the innermost muscle of the quads, stabilizes your kneecap and joint during walking or running.

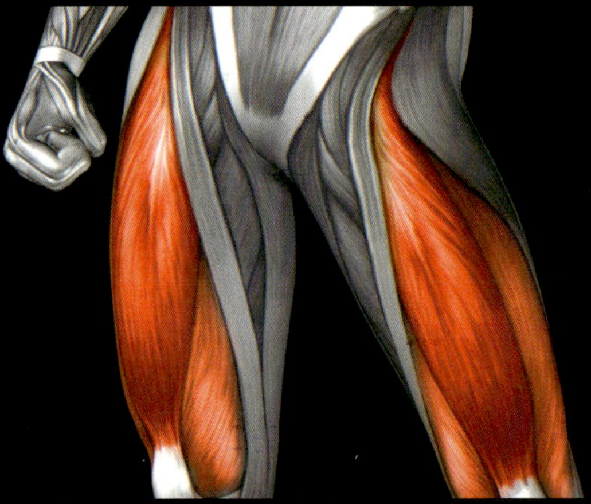

TONE YOUR QUADS

Having strong quads yields multiple benefits: your quads help to stabilize and protect your knee and hip joints, strengthen your bones, and increase muscle mass (which will help your body to burn calories more efficiently). And any endurance activity (in fact, just about any physical activity), such as walking, climbing, or running, relies on strong leg muscles. Here are three effective exercises to target your quads that require no extra equipment.

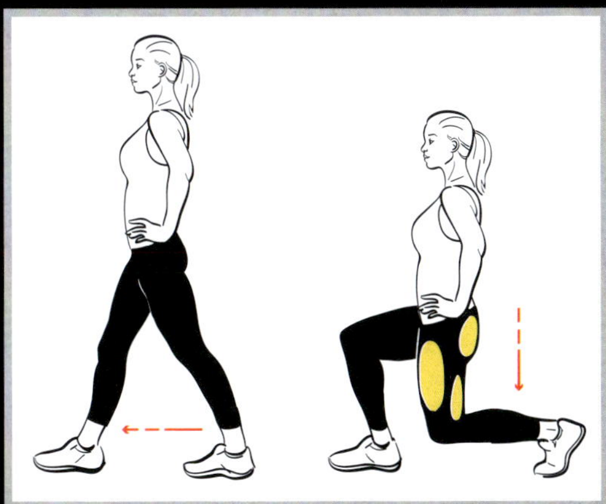

A **STATIONARY LUNGE** The lunge is one of the best leg exercises around, working nearly every part of your lower body. This version places an extra emphasis on your quads.

HOW Stand with your feet hip-width apart. Take a large step forward with your right foot. Keep your back straight and your right foot flat on the floor, and lower straight down until your right thigh is parallel to the floor. Hold for a count of two, and then slowly rise. Repeat for the desired reps, then switch legs.

B **NARROW-STANCE SQUAT** Like any squat, the close-stance squat will strengthen your entire lower body, with an added emphasis on the quads and outer-thigh muscles.

HOW Stand with your feet slightly closer than hip-distance apart. Keeping both feet completely flat on the ground, squat as low as you can. Hold the bottom position for a few seconds before returning to the top to begin the next rep.

C **WARRIOR II POSE** The series of yoga stances known as the Warrior poses calls for you to hold a lunge position. Warrior II stretches and strengthens the legs, while also building stamina.

HOW Stand with your feet facing forward and your legs wide apart. Turn your right foot 90 degrees so that it points straight out to the side. Raise your arms out to your sides so they are parallel to the floor, and then lower until your thigh is also close to parallel with the floor. Hold for 30 seconds to a minute, and then release the pose. Turn to the left, reversing the position of your feet, and repeat on the opposite side.

TRY IT WEIGHT FREE

You don't actually need barbells, dumbbells, or weight machines to perform effective quadriceps exercises—you can instead use your own body weight to supply resistance. These body-weight quads moves also work several muscle groups at once, which can make your leg workout more efficient when you're short on time. Because they require no equipment, you can perform a complete lower-body workout just about anywhere, and they are ideal for those days when you can't make it to the gym, but want to maintain your workout schedule.

TOOLS of the TRADE

IMPRESS WITH THE LEG PRESS

Despite how much we use our legs every day, it can be difficult to strengthen or sculpt them to the level we desire, even at the gym. The leg press machine, which is found in most gyms, health clubs, and fitness centers, enables you to both build strength in your lower body and tone your muscles from ankle to hip—give it a try, and you'll soon see results in your quadriceps, hamstrings, calves, and glutes. The leg press is also a useful tool for evaluating an athlete's overall body strength from knee to hip. There are two types of leg press machines.

DIAGONAL OR VERTICAL SLED LEG PRESS In this version of the leg press, you recline seated below a sled that has weight disks attached and is mounted on two rails, and you push the weight upward with your legs.

CABLE OR SEATED LEG PRESS In this version of the leg press, you sit with feet hip-width apart and flat against a footplate. You bend your knees to 90 degrees. and then extend your legs until they are straight but not locked.

etiquette

FOCUS ON YOURSELF

No matter what level you might have reached in any given endeavor, there will always be someone more advanced. That, in part, is why the gym is a good place to better yourself—there are so many success stories all around you. But no matter how admirable any other person's physique or definition may be, remember not to stare openly at anyone working out or resting between sets. Conversely, if you see someone noticeably unfit or fumbling with the equipment, unless they're doing something unsafe, simply leave them to find their footing in the gym. Whether you're a fitness pro or a rank beginner, always be polite—and give others their space.

BEST EXERCISES

WEIGHT FOR IT

Want to work on your quads at the gym? You'll find plenty of options. Along with the leg press machine, most gyms offer leg extension and hack squat units. Free-weight exercises using barbells and medicine balls also give your quads a real workout. As with any resistance exercise, start with lighter weights, and work your way higher as your strength increases.

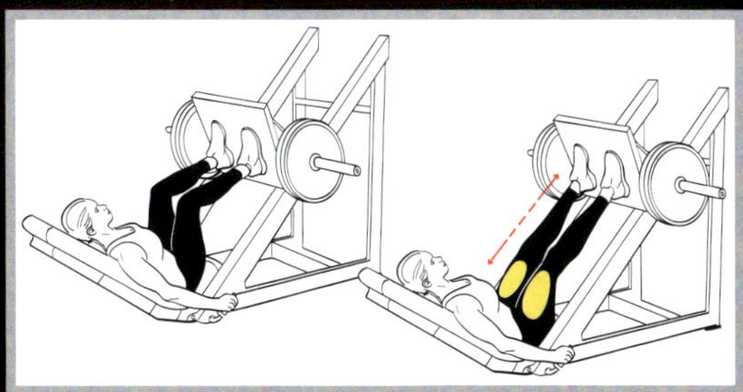

A **LEG PRESS** Leg presses are effective, but don't work with too-heavy weights, which may put you at risk for back problems.

HOW Sit on a leg-press machine with your back against the pad and your feet placed hip-width apart. Set the weight on a challenging, yet doable, resistance. Bend your knees to a 90-degree angle, keeping your feet flat against the footplate. Extend your legs until they are straight but not locked. Slowly return to the starting position.

B **BARBELL WALKING LUNGE** The exercise not only engages your quads, but also your glutes and hamstrings.

HOW Squeeze your shoulder blades, and place the barbell on top, making sure that the bar is resting on your muscles, not your spine. Grasp the bar with an overhand grip, step forward, and land first on your heel and then the forefoot. Keep your chest up, then lower your body by flexing the knee and hip of your front leg until the knee of your rear leg is almost in contact with the floor. With assistance from your rear leg, stand up on your front leg, and then lunge forward with the opposite leg.

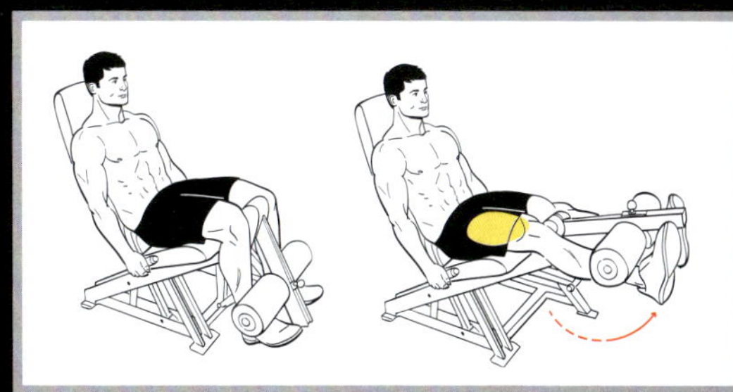

C **LEG EXTENSIONS** Another gym staple, the leg extension machine allows you to target the your quadriceps.

HOW Sit down on the seat of a leg extension machine, and hook your legs behind the padded bar. Adjust the bar so that it rests on your lower leg. Select a weight, and slowly lift the bar until your legs are almost straight, then lower your legs back down. Make sure to keep your back straight, and grip the handles on each side of the seat.

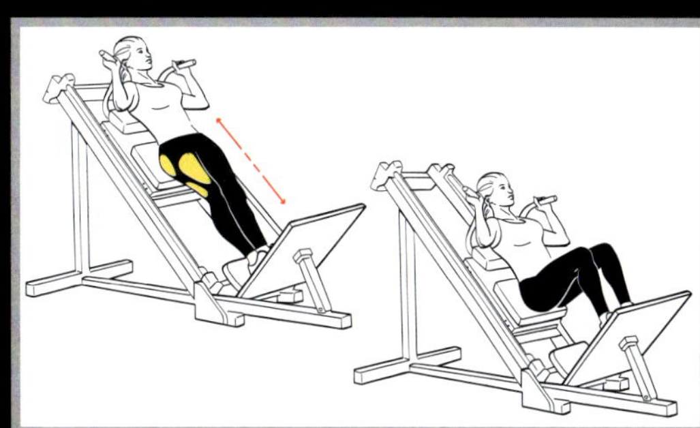

D **HACK SQUAT** Like the leg press, the hack squat machine allows you to effectively target your quadriceps.

HOW Lie back with your shoulders under the pads. Position your feet shoulder-width apart on the platform. Place your arms on the side handles, and disengage the safety bars. To get into the starting position, straighten your legs without locking your knees. Inhale, and bend your knees to slowly lower the unit until your upper legs are below parallel to the floor. Exhale, and push the sled with your heels to straighten your legs, and raise the unit back to the starting position.

KNOW YOUR... HAMSTRINGS

The group of muscles on the back of the thigh is known as the hamstrings. This group is made up of the semitendinosus, semimembranosus, and biceps femoris. When your trunk is fixed, the semitendinosus and semimembranosus extend the hip, and they flex the knee and rotate your lower leg inward when you bend your knee. When you take a step, the biceps femoris extends your hip and also flexes your knee and rotates your lower leg outward when your knee is bent. Along with the quadriceps, the hamstrings enable you to walk, run, jump, and squat.

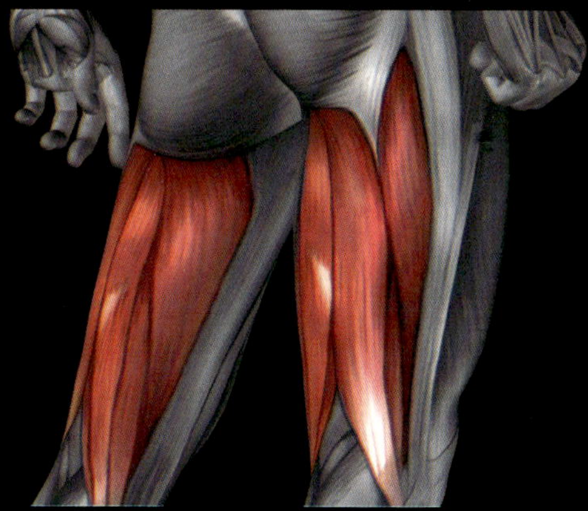

GUARD YOUR HAMSTRINGS

Many of us have jobs that require long hours seated at a desk; others spend a lot of time working or relaxing at their home computers. If this is the case, your hamstrings are likely to be tight—the result of muscles held in a static, shortened position. This tightness puts you at risk for hamstring injuries, knee injuries, and back pain. Hamstring injuries can also occur during athletic pursuits, such as jogging, soccer, baseball, volleyball, and basketball—as a result of over-training, falls, dehydration, and inflexibility. Support your hamstring strength work with a plan to keep these muscles supple. By creating a stretching routine involving both static and dynamic stretches, incorporating yoga or Pilates classes into your weekly routine, and focusing on training for balance, you will keep your hamstrings flexible and supportive.

HONE YOUR HAMSTRINGS

Whatever your athletic pursuit, to stay at the best performance level, you have to pay attention to your hamstrings. A regimen of exercises that target this group will help keep your legs strong and flexible. A typical plan is to start with two days of leg workouts per week, concentrating on the hamstrings work before you move on to more quad-dominant exercises. Start slow, and work up to the recommended sets and reps. With dedication, not only will you eventually be able to run faster, jump higher, and squat and deadlift a heavier weight, you also reduce your chances of sustaining a knee injury.

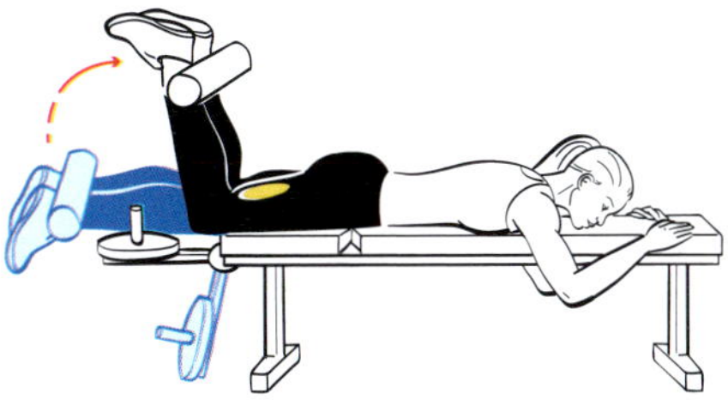

A **HAMSTRING CURL MACHINE** Lying leg curls work the hamstrings with particular emphasis on the biceps femoris. Perform three sets of 15 reps.

HOW Set a hamstring curl machine to a challenging, but doable, weight. Lie down on your stomach on the bench, and hook your ankles in place behind the padded leg rests. Draw your ankles toward your buttocks until your legs form a 90-degree angle. Slowly return to the starting position.

B **STABILITY BALL HAMSTRING CURL** This hamstring curl utilizes a ball to help raise your legs and hips off the floor. It precisely targets your hamstrings and also engages your hip and back muscles. Perform one set of 20 reps.

HOW Lie with your calves on the ball, arms by your sides, palms up. Raise your hips until your body forms a straight line from shoulders to heels. Bend your knees to roll the ball toward you until your feet are flat. Straighten your legs to roll the ball back, and then lower your body to the floor.

C **BOX JUMP AND SQUAT** Depending on your skill, choose a box between 15 to 30 inches (38–76 cm) high. Perform one set of 10 reps.

HOW Start in the squat position about a foot from the edge of the box. Power off both legs, landing in the middle of the box in a half-squat position. Return to the starting position.

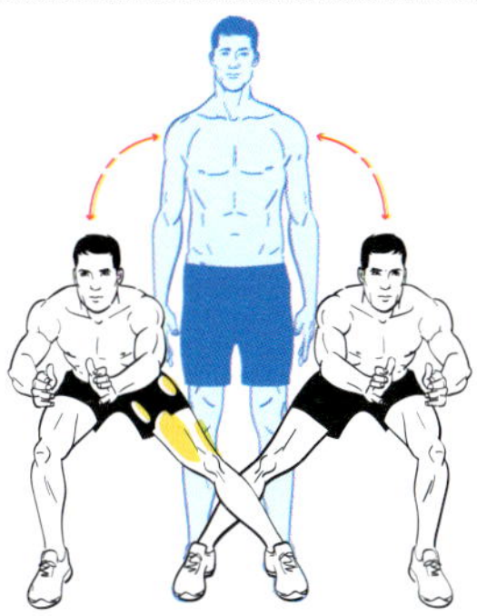

D **LATERAL SQUAT** Adding lateral movement to a squat improves rotational strength and flexibility in your hips and knees, while also refining your balance and coordination. Perform one set of 20 reps on each side.

HOW Start by taking a wide stance. Squat down to the right, keeping your weight on your right heel. Your left leg should remain straight. Sit as low as comfortable for one second, and then power up and alternate legs.

LEARN TO SQUAT

To really target your lower body muscles, including your quads, hamstrings, glutes, and core, the squat is a can't-miss compound exercise. It not only improves muscular strength and power, it also works almost every joint in your body while efficiently burning calories.

The basic squat is a great move no matter what your level of fitness, and there are many variations that increase its difficulty or add emphasis on particular muscles. You can also perform them anywhere with no special equipment.

The following squats use your own body weight for resistance, but you can add other weights, like barbells, kettlebells, or dumbbells, to lower your center of gravity and help you maintain balance.

Executing this exercise with proper form is essential, so keep in mind the following tips, which will help you get the maximum benefits from your squat reps.

HEAD UP Face forward with your head in a "neutral" position, meaning it should balance directly over your spine and not lean forward or be cocked to one side.

SHOULDERS BACK Keep your chest up and shoulders back.

ARMS BALANCED Extend your arms in front, parallel to the floor or hands entwined. You can also place your hands on your hips or bring them behind your head. The key is to keep balanced.

ABS TIGHT Engage your abs throughout the exercise.

KNEES IN LINE Make sure your knees are in line with your feet, and they should not come past your toes.

HEELS DOWN Keep your weight firmly on your heels—you should be able to lift your toes and wiggle them.

A **BASIC SQUAT**

WHY The squat is a great lower-body exercise that give you fast gains in size and strength.

HOW Stand with your feet hip-width apart. Slowly lower your bottom as you would to sit in a chair. While keeping your back straight and chin up. Lower as far as you can while keeping your knees parallel with your ankles, then slowly stand back up.

B **SUMO SQUAT**

WHY The sumo squat adds emphasis on the inner-thigh adductors.

HOW Stand with your feet wide, toes facing outward. Bend your knees and hips to slowly squat. Once you feel the stretch in the glutes and hamstrings, push up through your heels, and squeeze your glutes at the top.

C WALL SQUAT

WHY Wall squats have the same benefits as basic ones; practicing these will help perfect your form.

HOW Stand with your back against a wall, placing your feet about two feet in front of you and hip-width apart. Bend your knees, and slide your back down against the wall until your knees are at 90-degree angles. Hold for 30 to 60 seconds.

D BULGARIAN SPLIT SQUAT

WHY Split squats will help you develop balance and hip flexibility as they strengthen your lower body.

HOW Stand tall, and place one foot on a bench or similar sturdy platform. Keep your weight centered on your front foot and bend your legs to lunge. Bring your rear knee close to the floor, then drive up through your front heel to return to starting position.

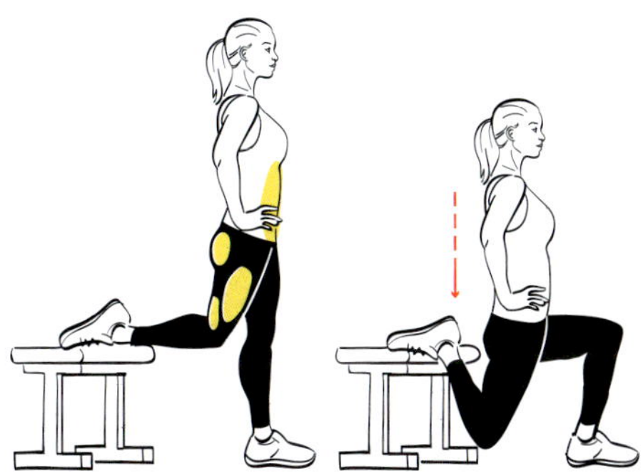

KNOW YOUR... CALF MUSCLES

Located on your lower legs are several muscles that move your ankles, feet, and toes. Giving your calves their characteristic shape is the gastrocnemius, the larger calf muscle. The gastrocnemius has two heads, which together create a diamond shape. Lying beneath the gastrocnemius is the soleus, a smaller, flat muscle. These muscles join to form the strong calcaneal tendon—also known as the Achilles tendon—and attach to the calcaneus bone in your heel. The gastrocnemius and soleus contract to flex the toes and also move your foot or toes to flex downward toward the sole, such as when you stand on tiptoes. On the front of your calves, the shin muscles, such as the tibialis anterior and extensor digitorum longus, are what bend the foot upward and extend the toes. All of your calf muscles also work to stabilize your ankle joint and feet and help you to maintain your balance.

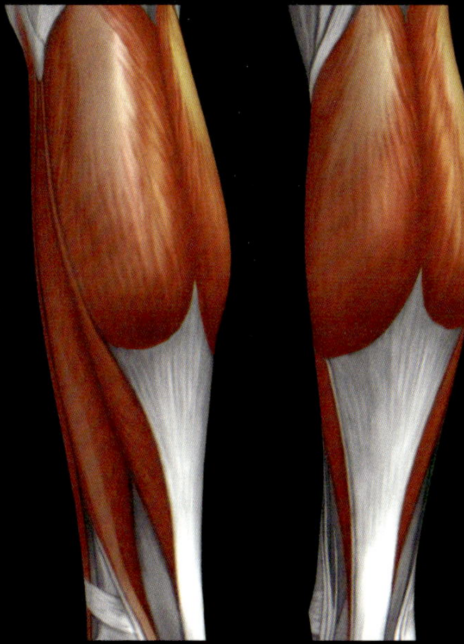

STAND ON TIPPY-TOES

Genetics ultimately determines just how much you can build the size of your calves, whether you are trying for the bulging appearance of a bodybuilder or the long, sleek look of a dancer. Whatever your goal, training your calf muscles will enhance your performance in many athletic pursuits.

HIKING, WALKING, AND RUNNING These pursuits are all excellent calf-strengthening exercises. Uphill walking or running is particularly beneficial—your calf muscles will really get a workout the steeper you climb.

RUNNING SPORTS Just look at the calves of a soccer player, and you'll be convinced that this kind of sport demands lower-leg strength. When you participate in running sports like soccer, tennis, lacrosse, field hockey, and basketball, you run, jump, and push off your calf muscles to accelerate or change direction quickly—and these kinds of moves will tone your calves.

DANCING Whether at a step or salsa class or pursuing ballet, dancing works calf muscles in ways few activities do, demanding that you step up and down or bend your knees and push off as you move from high to low positions.

TARGETED workout

CRAFT YOUR CALVES

To get a complete leg workout, incorporate calf resistance-training exercises into your fitness routine. Be warned, though: your calf muscles can be hard to work, mostly because the Achilles tendon comes into play when you lower or lift your heel. It acts similar to rubber band, transferring energy during the heel-lowering and heel-lifting phases of calf exercises, which means your muscles do less work. To counteract this effect, pause for about five seconds at the bottom of each rep and three seconds at the top.

Perform this routine about once a week. Gym newbies should perform just one set of each exercise. As your strength increases, work up to two and then three sets, resting for about two minutes between sets.

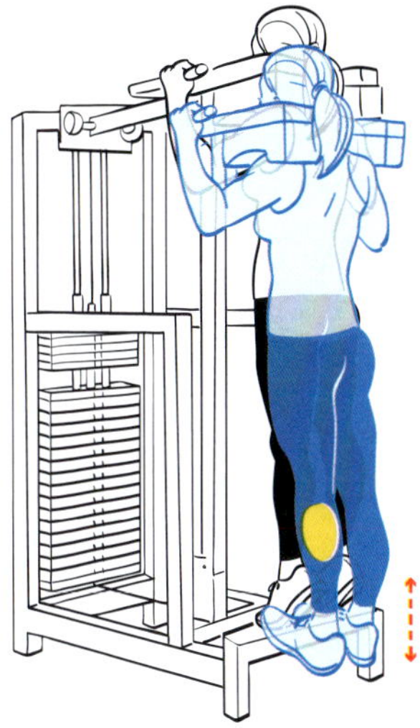

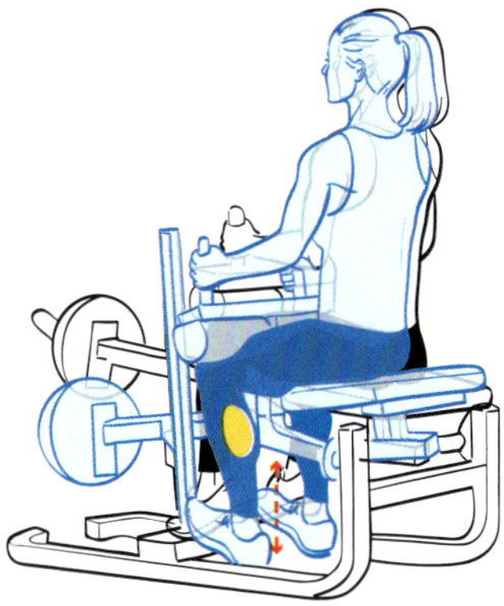

A **SEATED CALF RAISE MACHINE** A seated calf raise, by bending the knee, will relax your gastrocnemius muscles, placing more emphasis on your soleus muscles. Perform one to three sets of 12 reps.

HOW Sit at calf raise machine with your thighs under the leg pad and the balls of your feet on the foot rest, allowing your heels to hang off the edge. Slowly raise your heels up as high as you can go, pause, and then lower them.

B **STANDING CALF RAISE MACHINE** A standing calf raise, which you do with straight legs, will target the gastrocs more than the soleus muscles. Perform one to three sets of 12 reps on each leg.

HOW Stand on the footplate of a calf raise machine with your shoulders squared. Slowly rise up onto your toes, pause, and then lower your heels until fully extended. To work your calves one at a time, simply cross one leg over the other.

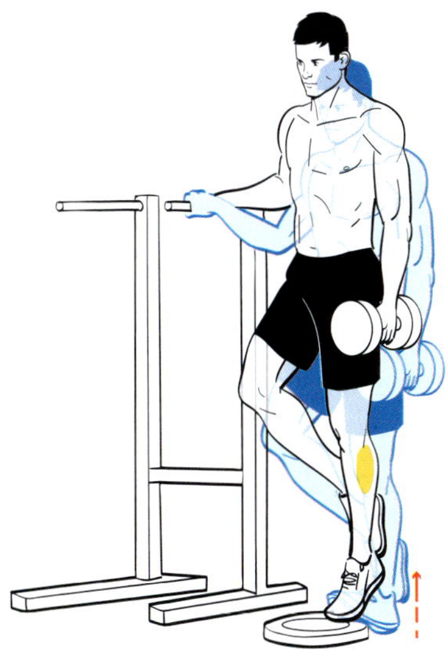

C **ONE-LEG DUMBBELL CALF RAISE** Standing calf raises place tension on both the lateral and medial heads of the gastroc muscle—resulting in thickness and definition. Perform one to three sets of 12 reps.

HOW Stand on one leg with your foot on a block, holding a dumbbell in the same-side hand, the other gripping a support for balance. Raise yourself up on to the ball of your foot, pause, and then lower your heel. Repeat on other leg.

GYM *etiquette*

TAKE YOUR TURN

Most of us live fast-paced lives, and when it comes to the gym, we want to get in, work out, get out, and get on with our day. When another gym-goer is using your favorite piece of equipment—or part of your workout circuit—you have a number of options. You can ask to work in, ask how many sets the user has left, simply wait, or find an alternative exercise.

GLOSSARY

aerobic Relating to activity that increases the body's demand for oxygen thereby resulting in temporary increase in breathing and heart rate.

augment To make something greater by adding to it.

bodybuilder A person who develops their physique through diet and exercise for competitions.

cholesterol A compound that is found in most body tissues, but a high proportion in the blood is associated with a high risk of heart disease.

cognitive Having to do with intellectual activity.

coordination The organization of different parts of the body to work together effectively.

deficiency A lack or shortage of something.

diabetes A disease in which the body's ability to produce or respond to the hormone insulin is impaired, resulting in abnormal metabolism of carbohydrates and elevated levels of glucose in the blood.

endurance The ability to sustain a prolonged stressful effort or activity.

etiquette The proper conduct observed in social life.

finesse Refinement or skillful handling.

glucose A simple sugar that is an important energy source in living organisms and is a component of many carbohydrates.

insulin A hormone produced in the pancreas that regulates the amount of glucose in the blood.

isolate To set something apart from others.

metabolism The chemical changes in living cells by which energy is provided for vital processes and activities.

neophyte A person who is new to something.

physique The form, size, and development of a person's body.

regimen A systematic plan to improve and maintain health.

resistance The power or capacity to resist, or push away.

salute A gesture of respect.

theory A belief or idea based on evidence.

FURTHER READING

BOOKS

Ashwell, Ken. *The Student's Anatomy of Exercise Manual.* Hauppauge, NY: Barron's Educational Series, Incorporated, 2012.

Delavier, Frederic, and Michael Gundill. *The Strength Training Anatomy Workout.* Champaign, IL: Human Kinetics Publishers, 2011.

Hutchinson, Alex. *Which Comes First, Cardio or Weights?: Fitness Myths, Training Truths, and Other Surprising Discoveries from the Science of Exercise.* New York, NY: Harper Collins Publishers, 2011.

WEBSITES

Activities

https://www.verywellfit.com/complete-beginners-guide-to-strength-training-1229585
Explore activities and suggested workouts for at-home weight training.

Safety

https://www.nationwidechildrens.org/specialties/sports-medicine/sports-medicine-articles/strength-training-for-teens
Check out tips for working out safely.

Weight Training

https://www.stanfordchildrens.org/en/topic/default?id=-weight-training-for-teens-1-2381
Learn about the importance of responsible weight training and discover the difference between weight training and bodybuilding.

INDEX